TAKE *Two*

LOVE ENDURES • BOOK ONE

SUSAN WARNER

TAKE *Two*

One

"'We need you.' Who falls for that line?" Natalie Tucker murmured to herself as she parked her car. The Banners knew how to play her like a flute. Having Grandma Banner call her and ask for help was the lowest of things to do. The worst part being that it had probably been Grandma Banner's idea.

"'Just take the file to him. He won't see anyone else,' they said," Natalie mimicked. The night before, her friend had cautioned her that this was a bad idea. However, Natalie was determined to prove she was over Jackson, and this favor to Grandma Banner would seal the deal and give her closure.

She would deliver the folder to Jackson and walk out of his life and start hers. A year was long enough to recuperate from a relationship.

If she had to describe Jackson, she would say he was a lot like chocolate. It looked good. It tasted good. In small doses, some people even claimed it was healthy. However, too much candy and you'd find yourself with a stomach ache, ashamed and alone in misery. That just about summed up Natalie's relationship with Jackson Banner, and the reason she had left the love of her life.

Natalie sat in her compact, non-airconditioned car and tried to compose herself. She looked in her rearview mirror to make sure she looked professional. Her dark hair was pulled back into a no-nonsense bun. Her makeup was neutral, emphasizing her naturally high cheekbones, but no makeup emphasized her large brown eyes or naturally long lashes. No, the point of this meeting wasn't to call any attention to her feminine attributes, it was about business.

Confident that her look complimented her tailor-made, dark blue suit, she reached over to grab her briefcase and mentally prepared to face the man she'd avoided for the last year, Jackson Banner. No better way to face the enemy than at his own house.

"I got this!" she said, in her best rah-rah voice.

As she got out of the car, she tried to assess what she could about the man Jackson Banner was today. Of course, his house was at the end of the block, set apart from the rest. It appeared privacy was still a big thing for him. That's fine. She liked her privacy too. In fact, her career had taken off in the last year due to dedication to work long hours and a self-enforced privacy so she wouldn't be distracted.

The house was distinctive as it appeared to be the only house that was under construction. Again, classic Jackson traits that suggested he thought his vision was better than the standard cookie-cutter house. His vision was good. She had vision. She had the vision to know she didn't need Jackson anymore.

The hot Florida sun beat down on the roof with missing tiles and sun-washed sides. She supposed the front lawn was green, but she couldn't tell with the large garbage bin sitting on it. As she walked by the lawn and toward the house, she could see his figure standing in the doorway.

"Natalie," he said.

Natalie didn't say a word. She waited for the languid warmth that was spreading through her body to subside. How could it be that this man still had this effect on her after what he did? Her mind was trying to get a grip on the situation, but her heart and body were having no part of the self-preservation techniques that only logic could offer.

"Jackson. I agreed to come out here, but my time is limited. So I'll say my part, and then I'll leave," Natalie stated. The tingles were still working themselves through her body, and she was holding onto the briefcase like a talisman.

She hoped she was presenting a strong front. The way to deal with Jackson was to set the tone. She was the woman in control here, and she was not going to fall for the Jackson appeal. She just needed to think about the picture her friend Gina had sent of a toad with Jackson's head on it. She could do this.

"Say your part? So you're here for—"

"I'm here because your Grandmother asked me to come." Oh yes, that line was firm and to the point. Natalie's inner self was giving her high fives on execution.

Jackson nodded. Natalie raised an eyebrow and grabbed the briefcase with both hands in front of her.

"Surely, you didn't think I was here for any other reason?"

"It doesn't matter what got you here, Natalie. I'll work with it," Jackson said in a low voice.

Shaking off the implied intimacy of that tone and those deep piercing eyes that called her like no other, she cleared her throat and continued on. "I sent you several emails, and I left some messages saying we need to talk."

"You did, and now we can," Jackson said as his mouth curved up in a small smile.

Natalie knew this wasn't going to be easy. Standing at the bottom of three worn steps, she had to admit Jackson Banner was a man in his prime. Dark hair that always had that I-just-ran-my-fingers-through-it look. A body that was sculpted for efficiency, and a gaze that had the power to mesmerize you. Natalie could feel her body start to lean towards him a bit, and there was a traitorous bead of sweat developing on her neck. She attributed to the hot weather and not the man before her.

In an attempt to pull herself together, she looked away from his face and took in his sculpted shoulders that led to lean arms and a chest that was covered by a dark blue shirt. He had on black, boot cut jeans, and dark shoes. The clothes clung to a frame that could have given Michelangelo's *David* a run for his money.

"Did you have the courtesy of reading any of my emails, or was that beyond you?" A cool breeze came by, and Natalie had to tuck an errant strand of her hair behind her ear.

"I never respond to personal matters via email," he said as his gaze tracked her hand at her throat.

Natalie could feel the blush coming, and there was nothing she could do about it. If he asked, she'd say it was the heat. She had to be imagining that Jackson wanted anything romantic to do with her. A year ago, the issue had been settled. She was not the one for Jackson Banner, and with time and space, she thought she had settled it in her heart. Jackson Banner wasn't the one for her.

She could feel his gaze on her throat and knew he was going to comment on the missing necklace that she had always worn for him, when she heard a small whining sound. She looked down and saw a small, grey and white, three-legged pitbull with a ball in its mouth. The dog hopped forward until it was between them, staring expectantly at Jackson.

Natalie cleared her throat and looked at Jackson. "Well, there is nothing personal I wish to discuss. I'll be—"

Then, before she could finish her statement, a crack of thunder ripped through the sky, and rain began to fall.

"It looks like you'll be coming inside. The good news is it's probably just a flash storm."

Natalie looked up and saw the dark clouds moving in and knew she didn't have a choice in the matter if she didn't want to get soaked. For a moment, she wanted to say that Jackson had planned this, but she knew he didn't have that kind of power. It was time for her to face this obstacle and put it firmly behind her.

She started up the steps and then gave him a long look as she stood on the porch. "I can stay out here and wait for the storm to pass."

Jackson stepped aside, and the dog went into the house first as if this was a routine for them both.

"Come on, Natalie, I've never known you to back down from a challenge. Come inside."

Natalie looked at him and heard the rain picking up. She sighed and then walked into the house as she threw over her shoulder, "I don't run from challenges, but I don't start something I know I can't win, either."

"You should know you'll always win with me," Jackson said.

Natalie ignored the comment and looked at the dog.

"If memory serves me correctly, you don't like pets," Natalie said, trying to project her voice and not let the uncertainty that was seeping into her show.

"People can change Natalie."

"Sometimes," she murmured. "Why is he carrying the ball?"

"Obi is always open to playing with whomever."

"Obi, as in, the master teacher?"

Jackson smiled. "Yes, that one. Obi's ready for the opportunity to play whenever it comes. I thought I could learn a lot from him. If a dog understands that concept, maybe he could teach it to me."

"Yes, well, I hope you two live in male bliss. Hopefully, the storm will blow through, and I'll leave this bachelor pad to you both," Natalie said, as she walked into a large room with hardwood floors. The room was divided by the strategic placement of furniture throughout.

To the immediate right was an old fashioned bar with two barstools in front. She walked over to it and began to shrug off her business jacket. Underneath she had on a cream-colored blouse and was thankful she hadn't worn anything heavier or he would surely see the sweat under her armpits. To face Jackson, she'd donned her sturdiest high heels. She would try to even out the height distance from her five foot nine to his six foot two.

"To not talk about us is just delaying the inevitable," Jackson said.

"You're entitled to be wrong." She draped her jacket on the barstool and turned to face Jackson.

She could feel his eyes watching her every move. "You could have given me your jacket. I still have manners, Natalie."

"Why? I won't be here long enough for us to do all the pleasantries." She placed her briefcase atop the stool and pulled out the folder. This wasn't the way it was supposed to happen. She was supposed to come to give Jackson a message. He was supposed to feel and say nothing about the past or even mention there might have been a past at all, and she would go back home to her life.

Jackson was once again rewriting the rules and making things difficult. What did she expect from a man who was so stubborn his Grandmother had to reach out to his ex in order to give him a message?

It appeared that about a year ago, Jackson had decided to take a hiatus from the company and start a little consulting business on the side. It functioned the same as the original, and just like the original, it was a success. Jackson started businesses like other people started hobbies. The Banner's knew whatever Jackson worked on paid off in the end. He was referred to as "the King," and the title fit in more than one way.

She turned with the folder in her hand, only to find he had moved to the other barstool. Sitting down, Jackson looked like pent-up power waiting to explode. This close up she could appreciate that the breadth of his shoulders were wider than before, and while he had worked out when they were together, there was a leanness about him that a man got from manual labor rather than visiting a gym.

Sitting on the barstool, she could see the slight pull of his shirt around his flat stomach. She jumped when another crack of thunder echoed from outside. Inside she thanked the higher power that existed for pulling her out of a rabbit hole of possibility and times she couldn't have with Jackson anymore.

"I'm here, you're here. Let's talk," he said.

Natalie pushed the folder towards him. "Anything we need to talk about is in this folder from your Grandmother."

Natalie turned away from Jackson and took in the room. There was a large, seventy-two-inch TV screen sitting on a console that looked like it came straight from a high-quality store. Then the rest of the room was filled with what seemed to be old, second-hand furniture. She wouldn't have been surprised if some of the furniture had come with the house. This wasn't the Jackson she knew. On top of being gifted in business, he had a sense of style she always liked but could never really afford.

"Why don't you just tell me what's in the folder, and then we can talk about the important stuff," Jackson said, as he pushed the folder back to her.

Natalie hoped her eyes weren't narrowing with the agitation she felt right now. "Don't play Jackson. You know why I'm here. You are needed at home."

"Who needs me, Natalie?" he asked with a smile.

Natalie leaned towards him on the bar. "Let's be clear. Your Grandmother has been and continues to be the kindest person to me personally and professionally. I'm here because she said you were acting like a two-year-old and had decided to take a hiatus from the company."

"I wasn't on hiatus. I needed a tactical retreat. It took a little longer than I thought. By the way, the cream shirt really highlights your hair."

Natalie pursed her lips and let out a deep sigh. "Focus, Jackson. You can call this away-time whatever you want. Your company needs you, and your Grandmother would appreciate it if you would show some interest in your birthright."

"Did I ever tell you that when you're passionate about something, your eyes sparkle?"

"You can't be serious!"

"Yes, Natalie, I finally am very serious. The last year has taught me that what matters most are a person's priorities."

"That's what I'm trying to get you to see. Your heritage should be your priority," Natalie retorted. "You need to go home and make the company right."

"Was that the only reason you came? Did you wonder about me?"

Natalie wanted to sit back, but retreating from Jackson now wasn't an option. She wasn't sure what game Jackson was playing, but she knew she couldn't go down memory lane with him.

"Why would I wonder about a man who didn't want me?"

"Wanting you has never been the issue."

"What game are you playing here, Jackson?"

He leaned back and shrugged his shoulders. "There's no game Natalie. I made a mistake."

It was as if the air had been sucked right out of her. Natalie sat back and gave Jackson a hard look. She paused, trying to find the right words. "We are not doing this, Jackson."

"Doing what?"

"Going down memory lane and reliving the past, and trying to find out what went wrong," Natalie said stiffly.

"You're right, we're not. I have no interest in the past at all. Only the future."

"Jackson, your Grandmother is seventy-eight. Maybe you don't understand what's going on."

Jackson shook his head. "I know. Over the last year, every family member who thought they knew how to run a company has taken a go at it. As a result, they have inconsistent results. They don't deliver on time, and what they do deliver they can't always support. Project Management is not the walk in the park they thought it would be."

Natalie swallowed, unsure of what was going on. "Okay, so you do know what is going on, then why am I here, Jackson? You know the financial straits they're in. It's not like you to ignore family."

"I'm not ignoring family. In fact, if you hadn't shown up in the next two months, I would have gone back."

Natalie sputtered. "You would have gone back—"

"It was only a matter of time before Gran called you. She was out of options."

Natalie put up her hands. "Hold on one second. Are you trying to tell me that you've been away for last year waiting for me to show up? How naïve do you think I am?!"

Natalie stepped off of the barstool and grabbed her jacket.

Jackson stepped in front of her. "I made a mistake. A year ago, I made a mistake. I didn't know it until a year in. I had come out here to get you out of my system. It didn't work."

"Well, I'm sorry I was a cramp in your life!" Natalie pushed past him and went to the door. She pulled it open and stepped onto the porch. She looked at the rain and thought if anything, she was in the middle of the storm, not the end. It didn't matter. Nothing mattered right now but getting away from Jackson. He was crazy. He was insane. What man puts his company at risk for a year. If he was even to be believed.

"Nat don't go," Jackson said from behind her. She was thankful for the rain, it hid the tears that were pooling in her eyes from hearing him say his nickname for her.

"I delivered the message, so my debt is cleared."

Natalie stepped into the rain and was drenched by the third step. She could feel her bun slipping, and her cream blouse was plastered to her chest. She had been so desperate to leave Jackson she'd forgotten to put on the jacket.

"Nat, really, you don't have to leave."

Natalie turned and faced him, placing her briefcase above her head. "A year ago, I made a mistake. I recovered. Now I come here to fulfill a debt I owed to your Gran, and I find it's all a game? No, it's definitely time I left."

"Fine, if you want to do it this way, fine." He passed her with a few long strides, went to her car and pulled it open so she could get in. Natalie sat on the seat and tossed her suitcase to the side.

"Nat," he said quietly.

Natalie looked up to see what other foolishness Jackson would say, and he didn't disappoint.

"Go back and tell Gran you spoke to me, but hear me out. A year ago, I was a fool. You are and will always be the best thing that ever happened to me. Did I take a hiatus from the company, and now the company business is failing due to poor management, yes? It was a small price."

"Price for what Jackson?"

"A small price to get you here. I wanted you to know I want you back. Drive carefully, Nat. I wouldn't want anything to happen to you."

Natalie watched him jog back to the house. She knew this was totally crazy. She needed space. The farther away from Jackson she got, the better she would be able to think. How could she believe him?

Did she want to believe him?

She started her car and wiped the moisture from her face. She wasn't one to run from the truth, and Natalie wasn't about to start now.

Today's encounter proved she still had feelings for Jackson, but that didn't mean she was ready to give the man who had turned down her marriage proposal another chance to break her heart.

Two

Jackson watched Natalie drive down the block until he couldn't see the bug-green, compact car anymore. This wasn't the way it was supposed to go. He mentally kicked himself and went back into the house.

Obi was sitting in the middle of the room with the ball still in his mouth.

"Obi, we are going to have to up our game to get that lady."

A minute after he said no to Natalie a year ago, he knew he had made a mistake. He would've fixed it right then if she hadn't run off. Sixty messages later and six months, he had come up with a plan. It was madness. It was extreme. It was all he had because the thought of living without Natalie wasn't an option.

He knew she was at a hotel about thirty minutes away from him. Jackson gave her an hour before he texted her.

Jackson: Are you at your hotel yet?
Natalie: Yes, thank you. I left the folder look at it.
Jackson: It was good to see you.

Natalie: Call your Grandmother.
Jackson: Now that you're back, I will.
Natalie: Jackson don't play.
Jackson: It's paltry. It's not enough, but let me start with I'm sorry.

He picked up his phone on the first ring.

"Hello, Nat." Jackson could hear her breathing hard on the other end of the line.

"Jackson you've got to—"

"Hear me out. I don't deserve it but hear me out, Nat," he pleaded.

She let out a huge sigh. "It won't make a difference, but go ahead."

"The first six months when I realized you weren't going to return my calls, I had already walked away from the company. I didn't know how long I'd be, but I couldn't concentrate on anything but you. This may seem extreme to you, but I want to make sure I don't make the same mistake twice."

"Jackson, I want you to know I'll always care about you. You drive me crazy. You always do the unexpected, but you hurt me, and if a couple doesn't have trust, then what's the point?"

"Give me time to earn your trust back?"

"Jackson, I just got a promotion at the consulting company I'm at. I took the time to do this, but I have a big project waiting for me. I can't just stop my life on a whim because you have had an epiphany!"

"But if you had the time would give us a chance, give me a chance?"

"I suppose, but it doesn't matter because—"

"I'm your big project," he said.

"What did you say, Jackson?" she said in a low voice.

"Time was running out. I thought Gran would call you way before this. You and she were always close. When we parted she thought we owed you more and better for the way the breakup had happened. I thought about buying, Vision Consultants, the firm you were working for, but I figured that would just make you angry, so I contracted with your company to help with Connected Solutions, it seems we need a subject matter expert to enhance our team of Project managers. Where the company is now I'd want some fresh, experienced blood in the company. I'd need you to help me fix the company anyway, and you're one of the— Hello?"

Jackson looked at the phone and then held it back to his ear. There was nothing.

There was no doubt about it. She was not happy with the turn of events. None of this was in the plan. He picked up the folder and then walked out of the room to the master bedroom he had converted into his office. There was a pull out bed in the room and a large desk with three monitors on it.

Two of the screens came up with the figures he had been looking at for Connected Solutions and his company, Natural Processes. On the third screen was a picture of Natalie. He stopped and looked at it. He had taken it at the zoo. She was laughing and sitting on a camel.

Natalie wasn't what people would call a textbook beautiful woman. Her face wasn't a perfect oval but it was beautiful. She didn't have large eyes that pulled you in but she had warm ones that made you feel like you'd come home. He reached his hand out to trace her smile, but there was something about the way she gave everything without reservation. She was nothing like Sylvia.

Natalie didn't need beauty like Sylvia, his first wife, had because she had wholesomeness that went beyond looks. When Natalie smiled at him, he knew the smile was for him and not for the crowds. When Natalie kissed him, he knew he was the center of her attention.

Natalie was nothing like his first wife. Being married to Sylvia had been the best and worst thirty days of his life. Sylvia had been exotic in her beauty. She knew how to perform for the cameras and the people around her. She always wanted to be the center of attention. Sylvia had worked at making him feel on edge and jealous. He hadn't known then that she needed help, and when she died in a motorcycle crash, he realized the both of them had needed help.

Jackson had given thought to marrying but never to someone as nice as Natalie. He thought he only deserved to be with a woman who matched him and could protect herself against his single-mindedness when it came to business. He was selfish, manipulative, and if the rumors were true, he could even be demanding. Natalie was the antithesis to that.

Natalie was the kind one who offered to buy you lunch, the giving one who gave her gloves to the homeless, the patient one who always had time to listen to a person in need. In short, she was just too good for him.

"What am I doing?" Jackson muttered to himself as he dropped his head into his hands. He didn't deserve her, but when she was around, she made him think he could be more than what they said. He could be—

The bounce of a ball broke him out of his reverie. Obi was sitting at his feet, looking expectantly at him.

When Obi looked at the ball rolling away and then at Jackson, and Jackson didn't move, Obi laid down on the floor. Jackson reached down and patted his head.

"Not now, let's wait until the rain stops," Jackson said.

Jackson had first seen Obi at a fair six months ago. Obi was on the side, and no one at the adopt-a-dog tent was paying any attention to him. Still, Obi looked expectantly at everyone with his ball in his mouth. Jackson walked up to Obi, and as if on cue, Obi rolled the ball to him and walked over. When Jackson saw he was missing a leg and still wanted to play and had a good disposition, he was sold.

Jackson understood what it took to keep a light heart in the face of so many difficulties, and if this dog could do it, maybe there was hope for him.

"Yep, we're really going to have to up your game if we're going to keep Natalie." Obi looked at him and then curled into a ball.

"Okay, I'm going to have to up my game," Jackson amended.

Jackson turned back to his monitors and looked at the numbers until he started to see a pattern. He could see the inconsistencies in the timelines, the budgets, and the goals. He would make sure Connects Solutions hadn't fallen too far and then work on his own company, which had been rated in the top ten up-and-coming consulting firms.

Business, Jackson understood. It wasn't about feelings or could-have's, would-have's or anything intangible. Business was about the numbers. This had been his refuge for the last year. While he had basked in his accomplishments, they had been hollow. It was then he had come to a conclusion. Making money was second nature to him, but if he didn't have Natalie, there wasn't a point to anything.

Three

Natalie stood at the window of Sherry Banner's corner office and watched the employees in the company parking lot below. The building for Connected Solutions went up to twenty-five floors, and Connected Solutions owned them all. This building was one of many in the Silver Park, a small complex of buildings all owned by Connected Solutions. It was Sherry's vision to have a community, and she had built one for her company.

Natalie looked at the employees coming and going below, unaware of what appeared to be impending doom. She had scheduled an appointment with Sherry to talk to her about Jackson. Maybe if they put their heads together, they could figure something out.

There had been a time when coming to this office had been one of the highlights of her day, but today it was obscured by a manipulative grown man who didn't want to accept—

"I'm glad you're here so early, Nat," Jackson said. "We didn't get to finish talking about things after the phone line dropped, but that's okay because—"

Natalie turned to see Jackson Banner standing in the doorway in full, corporate regalia. Oh yes, there was a reason they called him the king, and today he looked every bit of it. He had some folders in his hand, his jacket was unbuttoned, showing off a tapered waist in fitted pants that graced muscular legs. All of that was topped off with a gorgeous smile. She held her hand up, and he stopped talking.

"We were not cut off. I hung up."

Jackson laid the folder on the nearby desk and nodded. "I figured."

"Jackson, what are you doing?"

"I think they call this begging and pleading."

Natalie gave a small smile. "Most people beg and plead on their knees."

Jackson spread out his hands. "I was on my knees figuratively when I asked your company for you. I could have bought the company, but I'm trying to do the right thing."

"This is the worst attempt I've ever seen of a person trying to get back in another's good graces."

"I'm sure it's because I don't have any practice, and I'd like you to take that into consideration."

"Jackson—" Natalie said wearily as she looked away.

Jackson walked up to Natalie and lifted her chin to look at him. "Nat, you're right. I deserve nothing. I definitely don't deserve a second chance with you, and I'm not asking for any guarantees. I just want you to stay with me on this project, and let's see where it goes."

"And when it goes nowhere?"

"If by the end of this project, you still feel the same. I will give you whatever you ask, even if it means never seeing you again."

Natalie rolled the words over in her mind. It seemed so logical, but her heart shuddered at the premise. Jackson could be callous and arrogant, but he was a man of his word.

"Your word, Banner?"

"As long as you don't avoid me or deliberately try to keep us separated during the project, yes, my word."

Natalie looked at Jackson, and the world stopped. This was one of those moments her mother warned her about. It was a time when you had to make a decision at the crossroads. Looking at Jackson, she also remembered her mother's last words. "Better to live to the fullest and get hurt than to regret what might have been."

"I'm promising that I'll be here and do my job, nothing more," she said. Jackson smiled and grabbed both of her hands in his. He lifted them, and Natalie looked at him and then at their joined hands.

Jackson dropped her hands and nodded. "Yeah, thanks, Nat. So let's get started."

Jackson went to the desk, opened the file, and started reading stats as he brought her up to speed on his findings.

Her contract was for three months, or until the project was done. She could do this. She would ignore those tantalizing tingles that ran up her spine as he spoke. She wouldn't get pulled in by the excitement that lit up his eyes as he looked at the problem before him. She wasn't sure how she could still be attracted to a man who had hurt her, but she was going to use this time to her best advantage. She would take this time to find a way to cure herself of Jackson Banner. Then just as she was trying to figure out how to deal with one Banner, another came in. Sherry Banner, known to everyone in the company as Gran.

Natalie often joked about it with her friend, Gina, but the Banner's reminded her of prairie dogs. When there was a problem, they would look out for each other, but when nothing threatened them from without, they could argue like the best of them. Today looked as though it was going to be one of those days.

Sherry Banner walked into the office. At five foot eleven, with a swimmer's build and gray-streaked hair, she was a woman who was still in her prime.

"So, you decided to stop feeling sorry for yourself and come home to work?" Sherry said as she embraced Jackson. When she pulled back, her lips were pursed in disapproval. "I really couldn't believe you would make me send Natalie."

Natalie cleared her throat. Sherry turned towards her and smiled.

"Thank you so much for getting Jackson back where he belongs."

"I'm here now, Gran," Jackson replied.

Sherry's brows rose. "You are, but is it enough? You know Jackson, that's always been your problem; you're cold as a fish or as passionate as an artist. We all know that Natalie is the only middle ground you've ever stuck with, and you messed that up too."

"Gran—" Jackson protested.

Sherry looked between Natalie and Jackson. "Well, I hope you're not expecting me to watch my tongue about your silliness? I'm too old for these shenanigans. You should have just got on your knees and begged like other men do, but no, you had to come up with some elaborate plan. Really Jackson who risks everything to get a woman back instead of just talking to her?" she said as she waved her hands in the air. "Kids, always taking the long route. Well, I'm not getting any younger, fix this up with some speed because your loving relatives have decided how to split up the company and kick you out of being CEO."

"What?" Jackson said, confused.

Natalie closed her eyes, listening to the drama unfold. She was forgotten in the room as Gran laid it all out for Jackson.

"Let me tell you plain so you can't say I told you wrong. While you were deciding whether you should listen to your heart or not, your family sent an invite to the board members to vote on removing you from your CEO spot. They claim you're not fit. You abandoned the post to open another company in the same field, and you let this one slide so you could buy it out at a cheaper rate. Now I know you. You probably started the other company because you were bored, but others are not as understanding, nor do they need to be."

"Did you decide to vote with them too?" Jackson asked.

"Not yet. I wanted to find out if you had any sense left. Well, Natalie has brought you back. You need to get to work." Sherry looked at Natalie with a smile. "Thank you, child, for getting the stubborn boy. I'm tired. I have to go volunteer at the hospital later, and I want to be fresh for the kids. Jackson make it better."

Natalie groaned to herself as she looked at Jackson sinking into his thinking mode and Gran walking out the door. As she opened the office door, everyone could hear Gran call out.

"The King is home; let's hope he can save it."

Walking the halls of Connected Solutions was eerie. Four years ago, she was a fixture around here as much as Gran and Jackson. She had already been told she would be in her old office. On top of that, she would have her secretary back, Catherine Ling.

Catherine was in her mid-seventies. She was proudly Chinese, and at five foot four had a very big opinion on everything. In fact, Natalie couldn't recall a single time that Catherine didn't know someone who had gone through the same situation that was being talked about.

Natalie walked to the other end of the hall to the corner office and saw her name on the outside. When she walked into the outer office, Catherine was sitting at the desk looking over her red, cat-eye shaped glasses. Catherine crooked her finger, and Natalie leaned in to hear her.

"The round man is inside your office and welcome back." With those words, she sat back in her chair and cleared her throat. "You know I had a cousin who broke up with his woman. It was a dumb move, but he was able to make it better. I hope Mr. Banner has the same luck. I can give him the cousin's number, maybe."

Natalie smiled. "Jackson doesn't need any help."

"Call me if you need anything," Catherine mouthed.

Rob Littleson, also known as the round man, was one of the people Natalie had hoped had moved on. He was the lead Project manager on all large projects when Natalie or Jackson wasn't available. She knew Rob didn't like her and had come very close to suggesting that her placement at Connected had more to do with her relationship than her skillset. She took a deep breath and let it out, she just needed to get through the meeting.

"Hello, Rob," Natalie said with a bright tone. She tried not to take offense that he was sitting on her desk, finishing up a powdered donut. Natalie tried not to see the powder crumbs rolling over his stomach, which was covered by a blue shirt whose buttons were barely staying in their loops as they stretched across his extended abdomen.

"So the dynamic duo is back, I hear?" he asked, and she could feel him looking at her from head to toe. She didn't flinch.

It was true that Rob was big but all in all, he was a decent looking man. He was in his late forties and was always dressed to the nine's. Natalie didn't know how he did it, but it didn't matter whether it was summer, spring, fall, or winter. Rob was dressed for success.

He had brown hair with blonde tips that made him look younger than what he was. He had small, beady eyes that reminded her of a rat the way they went back and forth. All of that, coupled with his perfect teeth that were unnaturally straight, and he was a person she would never turn her back on.

"I'm here on a contract," Natalie said. She didn't tell him to get off of her desk. Instead, she went right past him to the small refrigerator in the corner and pulled out a bottle of water. Then she took a seat at her desk, which forced Rob to move to see her. "Just to be clear,

Gran and Jackson asked me to come because things are not going well."

"It's a small issue, and I'm taking care of it," Rob protested.

"I have no idea, either way, Rob. What I do know is the Banners called me in. I'll be looking things over. When it all comes down to it, the person who will be doing the saving is Jackson."

"So everyone is waiting for the King to save us," he sneered.

"We all need him if we want Connected to see the next quarter," Natalie said. Rob didn't seem surprised by the news. In fact, he was more obsessed with Jackson coming back than anything else.

"Banners will look out for Banners," he said quietly. "You should remember that." Without waiting for her to reply, Rob walked out of her office.

Natalie looked around her office and sighed.

"Oh yeah, it's just like the good old days, she muttered to herself.

Four

"I need your help," Jackson said as he strode into Gran's office.

"It's true you do need help, but not mine."

"Gran, I messed up."

"We all agree on that."

Jackson felt like he was a kid again. Gran was everything he hoped to be when he got older: feisty and wise.

Jackson let a smile spread across his face as he watched Gran take a seat. If this plan was going to work, he needed Gran.

"This was extreme, and it upset her," Gran said.

"I was desperate."

"You hurt her Jackson. Women aren't businesses that you can find the right formula or pay the union for something. Natalie is a complex woman, and you've hurt her." Gran sat back in her high back leather chair. "To add insult to injury you've trapped her in a contract to help you only proving you are a worthless, sneaky, no good—"

"I think I've got the idea, Gran!"

Gran smiled sadly. "I'll help you as much as I can, but you should be prepared that you may not be able to fix this."

Jackson nodded. "I know there is a possibility, but I'm not entertaining it, and instead, I'm investing in my contingency plans."

"Ahh, well, if nothing else, it will be entertaining to watch her educate you," Gran murmured.

"Natalie just needs to be reminded of what made us so great together. I can do that."

"I am curious about something."

"Yes?"

"All of this effort and hoopla for Natalie now. If the question of marriage comes up, do you know what you'll say?"

"I'll handle it." Jackson wasn't ready to bear his soul to Gran on that one. Probably because he didn't know what the answer was. "When Nat's ready to listen. I'll explain it all, and she'll understand."

Gran waved her hand in the air. "I don't know about her understanding, but I know she's been working and making a name for herself. She barely dates, and she's considered one of the best operations people out there."

Jackson grinned. "Of course, she is."

"She's on the path to opening up her own place, Jackson."

"And?"

"And I'm telling you, so you don't foolishly think the company or your money will have any weight with winning her back. A year ago, you had a company that was doing well, and you could offer her a position in it. Now, a year later, companies are offering for her. What I'm saying is materially, you have nothing she can't get, so make sure you're ready to give yourself this time."

Jackson walked out of Gran's office and made a beeline to Natalie's. With all the foreboding tones of doom and gloom, he needed to start right away. He made it down the hall in record time to run into Catherine Ling, guarding the gate.

"Hello Jackson, what can I do for you?"

"Natalie?"

"She's with Mr. Littleton and—"

"No problem, I'll join their meeting."

"Oh, Jackson, but I think they are—" Catherine tried to talk to him, but he kept moving until he had knocked on the door and pushed it open. Rob was precariously perched on the desk, and for a moment, Jackson thought he saw Rob glower at him.

"Jackson, it's nice to see you back in the place again."

Jackson took his hand but didn't linger in the exchange. In fact, he gave Rob a nod and paused as if to think.

"Rob, perhaps you are just the right person that I'm looking for. I'm going to need someone to bring me a list of all of the projects that we are failing and have failed."

Rob looked over his shoulder at Natalie and then nodded to Jackson. Jackson kept on as if he hadn't seen the interaction.

"I'm going to visit some of our clients to get an idea of what their feeling is towards us, and to get some more business if they'll have us. I'll also need to finish packing my place and setting up here."

"You think you'll be staying here then?" Rob asked.

Jackson looked up until he caught Natalie's eye.

"I certainly will. Everything I want is here." Natalie held his gaze for a few seconds more and then turned away.

Rob cleared his throat and excused himself, saying he would get to work on the files.

Jackson watched Natalie shuffle some papers around on her desk. Then he walked up to the desk and placed his hand on top of hers.

"Nat, do I make you nervous?"

He heard her let out a sigh. "Let's just say this day hasn't been a run of the mill day for me."

Jackson traced the top of her hand with his pointer finger. "No matter what may or may not happen, I want you to know that professionally, there is no one I trust more."

Natalie looked up at him and smiled. "You know Jackson, that is the first time you've actually complimented me on my work."

He gave her a smile as he thought about it. "Wow, that's pretty bad. Considering how much I admire your work. Okay, I can see I've got my work cut out for me."

Natalie pulled her hand back and looked away, trying to cover her smile.

"I was wondering if you'd do me a favor," Jackson said.

"Of course, I'm here to help you."

"You know he's Prince Charming with a dark heart," Gina said as she ate.

Natalie looked at her roommate across the kitchen table. She regretted the fit of anger that had made her come home and tell Gina the favor Jackson had asked of her. Gina worked at the consulting agency with her. When Gina took a liking to you, she'd defend you to the end. Today was no exception. The recipient of Gina's wrath was Jackson.

No one would know it, as Gina was a petite five foot five, but to date, nothing had ever gotten between Gina and food. With red hair, an opinion to share with everyone, and by the way she was aggressively cutting up her pancakes, Gina was just warming up her wrath.

"So do you want to explain to me again how the dark prince managed to saddle you with his dog?" Gina said as she slathered her pancakes with syrup.

Natalie let out a sigh. "He asked me for help so he could settle in. He's moving, and he wants to visit some clients. It would be stressful for the dog."

"Uh-huh. So Prince Warbucks couldn't afford to get a person to watch the dog or put him in one of those fancy hotels?"

"Gina, it's a small dog."

Gina popped a strip of bacon in her mouth and then waved the second strip at Natalie. "Little dogs or big dogs they all need someone to clear up after them."

"I know."

"If I had wanted to do that, I'd have had kids. At least there's a chance of return on investment with them."

Natalie looked at Gina inhaling the food on her plate and smiled. "Well, I'm not sure you're ready for motherhood, but they say you should practice on a plant or a small animal first. Jackson will be here soon. When you see Obi, you'll see he's not going to be a problem at all."

"So what's the deal, Natalie? Are you doing this for the old woman? Or is this something else?"

Natalie picked up her coffee cup and took a sip, avoiding the question. "For right now, it's a job. Professionally I can do this. The assignment is good. The pay is better. They don't call him the "King" for nothing."

Gina reached over and plucked a strip of bacon off of Natalie's plate. "You have a plan for him, right? I mean, you're not going to fall for the 'I'm sorry,' just because he's rich and hot?"

Natalie raised her eyebrow. "I know Jackson. No, I wasn't planning on falling for anything, but I have to say it sounds different when you say it, Gina."

"Look, I'm just saying. He's a Banner. They have a reputation."

Natalie nodded. "I'm not looking for anything except finishing the job. I'm going to take it one day at a time," Natalie replied.

The bell rang, and both women turned towards the door. Gina popped the rest of Natalie's bacon strip in her mouth and nodded towards the door.

"No worries my pretty, I'll answer the door," Gina said in a fake cackle. Natalie looked at her plate and realized breakfast was over. She wouldn't be able to finish her meal anyway. Instead, she gathered herself and placed the dishes in the sink. She heard the telltale sign of a squeaking toy, and she knew Obi had brought his ball. Moments later, Jackson was in her kitchen with a smile and what appeared to be a grocery bag filled with Tupperware.

She looked up at Jackson and then down on the floor at Obi, who was staring up at Jackson as if he were the only person in the world that mattered.

"Where's his crate?" Natalie asked.

"Crate?"

"Yeah, you know that thing you put dogs in at night? According to some dog specialist, it's good for them because they have their own space."

Jackson put the shopping bag down and picked Obi up in his arms.

"Don't say words like that around him. He's sensitive. I don't have a crate because I wouldn't want someone to put me in one, so I didn't get him one."

Natalie looked at Jackson incredulously. "Now, you decide to be considerate?" Pointing at the shopping bag on the table, she looked at Jackson. "Do I even want to know what's in that bag?"

Jackson smiled. "His food. I've put the dates on it so he doesn't eat the same thing twice in a row. He likes variety."

Natalie was about to give him her opinion about a dog's right to choose, when she heard Gina snorting in an attempt not to laugh. "Oh, I can so see how this is going."

Jackson looked over his shoulder and nodded. "I'm so sorry, I didn't catch your name, and I certainly didn't mean to interrupt your breakfast."

"Didn't mean to interrupt my breakfast, you say? Oh yeah, that and the dog thing makes me think you were completely underestimated, but you have earned coffee if you'd like a cup," Gina said.

"Really, Gina!" Natalie hissed.

"Thank you. I'd appreciate it. I'm trying to make a good impression," Jackson said as he pulled out a chair at the round, wooden table and sat down. Gina served him coffee and then went to stand in the doorway.

"So, Mr. Banner, Natalie says you're leaving your dog here?"

He nodded. "I trust her, and this is on such short notice that I don't want to spook Obi. Besides, he likes her, so it seemed like it was a no-brainer. You don't mind, do you, Natalie? There's still time for me to make some other arrangements."

"No, I'm fine," Natalie said. "I'm sure it will be fine."

Gina walked by Natalie to get to the sink and murmured, so only Natalie would hear. "Pride goeth before the fall. Tell him no."

Jackson finished the coffee and then stood up. "Thanks, Nat. I need to get on my way so I can get back."

"No problem."

Then Jackson reached into his pocket and brought out a piece of paper. "I just wanted to leave what I normally do with him. You don't need to, but as much as you can, that would be great."

Gina reached past her and took the list. "Got it." Gina whistled. "This is a pretty extensive list. Natalie and I were just saying that people who want kids should start with pets or plants."

"Umm, that wasn't quite the conversation but—"

Jackson shrugged. "I don't know about that, I think Obi is pretty easy to take care of."

Gina handed Natalie the list. When Natalie started reading it, she looked at Jackson more than once.

"Um, Jackson, really?"

"What's wrong?"

"It says if Obi doesn't eat his food, change the color of the bowl?"

"He's picky sometimes."

Natalie kept reading, and then she put the list down. "Well, I don't think I can do the last one."

Jackson looked confused. "Which is?"

"Obi gets the right side of the bed?"

"Do you sleep on the right?" Jackson asked.

Gina almost choked at the sink. Natalie wanted to reach out and shake Jackson. Where was the overbearing jerk she had met earlier? Was she really having a conversation about where a dog was going to sleep?

"Listen," Gina interjected, "I've got to go to work, so I'll leave you two new parents alone."

When Gina left, Natalie turned on Jackson. "I would prefer, if we are having a disagreement that we talk about it privately and not in front of Gina."

Jackson smiled. "Are you one of those parents that don't believe kids should see their parents argue?"

"One, I do believe children shouldn't be bothered, and two, we aren't parents!"

Jackson held out his hands. "Since we are setting ground rules. What's your relationship with Rob?"

Natalie had to do a double-take. "Jackson, I just got back to the company. Today was the first day I spoke to him."

"Yeah, well, I think it's best if we keep our distance from employees until I can do some more research."

"What are you talking about?" she said, unable to keep the irritation out of her voice.

"I'm saying that Connected shouldn't be in the shape it's in." Jackson leaned over and stroked Obi. "When I come back, we'll talk again. I'll have some more insight for us all."

"Insight? Jackson, what's going on?"

"I don't know yet, but I want to keep my options open."

Natalie looked at him stroking Obi. "You don't look all that moved by it. If you have these concerns, have you told them to your Grandmother?"

Jackson put Obi down and then took a sip of his refilled drink. "There's nothing to tell yet. Besides, if I even had a suspicion and I told Gran, you know what would happen. She'd clean house and protect her assets. That's a short term thought. I need to clean Connected, not just hold on to my position as CEO."

"Maybe I should come back later when this is done, Jackson."

"No, you are the only person I'd like to have with me during this."

"Because?"

"Because I trust you. The work that I think is going on here isn't your style."

"Maybe that's your problem, Jackson. You think you know me."

Jackson stood up and looked at Natalie. "I don't think. I know you, Nat. I know you're not going to make this easy for me. I know I have a long road ahead. To get started, I've got to be on my way, and then I'll be back to work on us."

"There isn't an *us* Jackson, so go along and take care of your priorities."

Jackson turned to Nat, who stood with her arms crossed.

"Okay, what did I do now?"

"It's your presumptuousness, Jackson. Listen, go take care of your business, and I'll take care of mine."

Jackson went to Nat. "Take care of our kid, and I'll

be back." He bent down and placed a quick kiss on her forehead. Then he left.

Obi padded after him, and when the front door closed, that was when she heard the first signs that Obi whined.

Their kid. If it was truly their kid, Jackson would be in deep trouble when he returned with the way Obi whined, their kid was about to get a serious education on discipline from their other parent.

Natalie was sitting at the kitchen table when Gina came home. She was just finishing up her dinner when Gina closed the door.

"What is that noise?" Gina asked.

Natalie leaned out and saw Gina at the door, and then she pulled out the earplugs from her ears.

"Hi, Gina,"

"Don't you 'Hi, Gina' me, what is that noise?"

"Well, I bought Obi a crate, and he has been moaning ever since."

"You've got to be kidding me?"

"No, I wish I was."

Gina smiled as she dropped her coat and then went to sit at the table. "You know I don't want to interfere with your parenting, but I would like to sleep tonight."

Natalie looked at Gina and grinned, and then Natalie looked at Obi. He was looking at them both from the crate. When she turned her back on him, he stopped whining. Natalie looked at Gina and shook her head while the both of them laughed.

"Is this going to be the way you tame the King?"

"I'm not here to tame the King. I need to do my part and leave." She ignored the sly smile of knowing that spread across Gina's face. Natalie had a plan. She wanted to finish this job. Get some closure in her life and then move on.

And the truth of it was if she could survive Jackson, she would be whole and unstoppable. She had a promising career, and everything else would come. She'd learn from her mistakes with Jackson and move on. It would be a closure and a rebirth all in one mighty swoop.

Then Obi whined. Natalie rolled her eyes, and Gina laughed.

"You know I think you are the best planner and project manager out there, but I think this may not work out like you think. I think Jackson may surprise you."

"Whose side are you on Gina?" Natalie asked jokingly.

Gina paused and gave Natalie a smile. "I'm on the side that looks out for your happiness."

Five

Natalie was sitting in her office, listening to the mellow sounds of classical music. She rested her head against the chair rest, trying to release the stress and strains of the day. Jackson had arrived earlier today and had sequestered himself in his office next door. He had closed the door and hadn't come out. At one point, Catherine asked her about Jackson's state in his office.

Catherine had stood in Natalie's doorway.

"You know he's working the wrong way. Taking on everything at once instead of digesting bit by bit. You know I had a cousin who did this, and he died. It was very bad, and he was about the same age as Mr. Banner."

"Jackson is a big boy who knows his limits," had been her reply. However, it was past six, and the only thing that had stopped her from going into his office was that she could hear him next door moving around.

Just when she was thinking about going over to check on him before packing up, she received a text on her phone. Concerned it would be her boss, she went to answer it.

Jackson: I just finished my ten-minute meditation, and I can see why you are such a huge fan of it.

Natalie: I didn't know you meditated?

Natalie looked at the text and re-read the lines a couple of times. She supposed Jackson had started to meditate after their breakup. When they were together, he used to joke and say that real men didn't meditate. She laughed to herself and again looked at the text. *Well,* she thought, I *guess some men do meditate.*

Coffee? Should she or shouldn't she? It seemed so innocent, but it was Jackson.

Natalie: You do know you are right next door?

Jackson: It's after-hours. I didn't want to just show up.

Natalie: I think it's a bit late to be wandering for coffee. Besides you've got a welcome back party to go to.

Jackson: How about I go get the coffee and bring it back. It's only a block away. Don't remind me about the party.

Natalie: You're a big boy. I'll be there with you.

Jackson: That's the only reason I'm going.

Natalie: Stop complaining. Get coffee.

Jackson: While we are talking about tonight. Can I pick you up?

Natalie: We'll talk. Coffee first, dark, no sugar.

Jackson: I remember. See you in ten.

Natalie got a little tremor in her stomach. She knew she was playing with fire, but that was part of the process, exposing yourself little by little and then becoming immune. She could handle Jackson, and it was coffee in the office. It wouldn't get much safer than that. Besides, while he was here, they could discuss him picking up Obi.

Jackson pushed his work to the side and took a deep breath. It was a beast not to just go next door, sit on the sofa Natalie had in the office and just bounce the day's events off of her. He knew he wasn't there yet. He hoped she'd let him get back, but he had to take it slow. Tonight Gran wanted everyone to know she approved of his return, and this get-together would do that.

Jackson wasn't a fan of get-togethers. It always meant someone was in trouble or about to be in trouble, and most of the time, it was him. He picked up his keys and clipped them onto his belt loop so he could swipe in and out of the building.

He didn't look in Natalie's office; instead, he went down the hall and out the main office doors to the elevator. Normally he would have jogged down the steps, but tonight he pulled out his phone from his back pocket and figured he'd make sure all business texts were answered so nothing would interrupt his evening with Natalie.

As he pushed the button for the elevator, it came to him like an epiphany. He was feeling in control and with direction more so than he had been in the last year. He had meditated today, a practice that he had taken up initially for Natalie, but now was something he used to center himself. Today's meditation was the first time in a while, he had opened his eyes and felt relief. Natalie was here, and he had a chance. True, he still had to fix Connected, but that was something he knew and understood.

He heard the bell of the elevator, and the doors opened. It couldn't be worse timing. He kicked himself for not taking the stairs.

Elizabeth Banner, his aunt by marriage, and the advocate of all things for his uncle Howard and their kids. Kids who, if the rumors were to be believed, were trying to oust him from being the CEO.

Elizabeth stepped out of the elevator first. On top of being a forthright woman, she was definitely what Jackson would call big-boned. Elizabeth was five foot ten with brown hair, and a solid build.

"I'm so glad we caught you. We think we should have a conversation with you."

Jackson thought of every excuse and permutation of what would happen if he said no, and none of them worked out well. He could see Howard holding the elevator door and smiling behind Elizabeth. Well, it was clear that Banner men preferred women with fight and boldness, and Elizabeth fit the mold exactly.

He looked at them all, and they were already dressed for the party, which told him whatever they wanted to say they didn't think they'd have enough time to have this conversation and then go to the party. How much time had gone by already?

"Hello, Aunt Elizabeth, Uncle Howard. I see you're ready for the party. I need to do the same, so we can talk later." He gave a nod to his cousins, Lori and Chris lingering behind their parents. Really they were all just standing behind their mother Elizabeth, who always led the way.

"I think you've made that pretty impossible, Jackson," Elizabeth said primly.

"I'd have to agree with her," Howard said resignedly. Howard was shorter than Elizabeth but built like a fire hydrant. He wore glasses and kept his hair short and spiky to offset the thinning that was occurring. He always wore dark pants and a pastel shirt with the sleeves rolled up to show off a gym body that he was very faithful too. Jackson had to give Howard credit, he had the Banner trait to be known in his chosen field. Banner men found a passion and then poured themselves into it, Howard's was children. His face was round and invited conversation, which was great for him because he had developed a reputation as a child psychologist who could reach any child. He wasn't any good at business but he was one of the best child psychologists in New York.

Howard was in his signature clothing this time; he had a matching dark jacket to go with his ensemble.

"Sherry is having this meeting tonight for you," Howard said.

Jackson never got over the way uncle called Gran, Sherry. Jackson thought his tone and familiarity made it seem like he was better or knew more than Gran. It was no secret that Howard had, on more than one occasion, made suggestions to Gran on how to run Connected, and she had all but laughed him out of her office.

"Gran is having a party, not a meeting and until she tells us why, her reasons are her own."

"It's obvious she's going to be supporting you for the CEO position. I don't know why, though. Certainly, she should see that you have a problem with commitment. It was probably the loss of your parents at an early age," Howard concluded solemnly looking at Elizabeth as she nodded her head in agreement.

"Howard, we don't have your background, so we don't see things quite the same," he replied. He had been preparing to do this at dinner, not in the third-floor lobby of the office. As the conversation had started, the rest of the family came out of the elevator.

Chris was tall with dark hair, brown eyes, and he looked like he was trying to grow a beard. He had recently gotten his MBA and had that know-it-all air about him. Jackson thought Chris was smart, but he was just book smart and needed some time in the trenches of business.

"Hey, Jackson, it's good to see you. I hear you've been looking through Connected. I'm sure you've looked at our international partner deals and see they are all doing well," he said with a smile.

"I did see that, Chris. I also saw those deals only make up about 12% of Connected's income," Jackson said as he turned to face the leader of this group, Elizabeth. Jackson knew Chris was upset Gran hadn't turned to him when the problems began in the company. Jackson remembered what it was like to want to prove yourself so much that nothing else mattered.

Jackson looked at his watch, his time was ticking, and Natalie was waiting.

"I heard you were able to get Natalie to come back. That must have been some package you offered?" Lori commented.

Just when he was about to respond, he saw a flash of curly hair on his right. It was Natalie going into the ladies' room. The horde at the elevator was so intent on him they hadn't noticed. A few moments later, he got the text.

Natalie: You're busy see you later.

Jackson's heart sank, he texted back quickly so as not to offend the familial horde before him.

Jackson: No really.

Natalie: I'll take a range check on coffee. Family first, employees later.

Jackson didn't have words for the frustration that was riding him now. He turned towards Lori, she was in her late thirties. True to the Banner trait, she had a specialty. She was the head of culture and languages in Connected. Lori was a lawyer by trade and a polyglot by passion. All the foreign deals and projects that Connect got were done by her.

Tonight she wore a little black dress and matching black, cat-eye glasses. Her hair was cut in a stylish bob, and she had on a pale lipstick so her skin wouldn't be so white by comparison. The running joke was that Lori stayed in the library so much her skin lost its color.

Jackson didn't say anything to her because Lori had just gotten divorced this year. He thought she was a little paler, and the shadows under her eyes were deeper. After being without Natalie, he thought she was a stronger person than people gave her credit for. In fact, if he thought there was no chance at all for him and Natalie to get back together, he didn't think he'd be able to hold it together even half as well as she did.

"She took the job before she knew I was here," Jackson parried back.

Lori gave a slight smile. "Well, this should be

entertaining, at least. Did you advise Gran that it would be prudent to sell some assets until we get the rest together?" Lori said as if it was a fact.

"What would you suggest Lori, that we get rid of the international contracts? She won't consider selling anything domestic. Our Domestic business is what started this company, and as long as Gran and I are at the helm, it will be the driving force of the company."

Jackson saw Chris's face tighten, and Howard shake his head before looking away.

"Jackson, you've been away. We need to do something," Elizabeth said, folding her hands across her chest, looking annoyed. "It's time to consider that we may need some new blood in this new age. Have you considered that?"

Jackson took another glimpse at his phone and tried to focus on the situation at hand, which was his barracuda family who wanted him to fall on the sword so they could take over. He had no intention of doing so. All he needed was some time, Natalie, and a plan. He could fix this.

Family dynamics for Banner's were an odd thing. They fought like cats and dogs but pulled together for the greater good, despite their personal opinions. Or at least Jackson thought that would have been a given until he saw the slow bleed in Connected. At any rate, until he discovered otherwise, he was going to do what all other Banner's had done before him. He was about to trust his greedy family to have his back.

"Okay, we've got to get some things straight. There will be no new blood heading Connected," he said firmly.

"You didn't even give it a good try, how can you say that," Elizabeth grumbled.

"I can say that because I'm staying. So you will all have to deal with the old fox you have," he said. "Next, I'm trying to work on getting Natalie back, so we will be playing everything by ear. I'm getting all the information I need to fix the company, and get Natalie back in my life."

Chris shook his head. "I think it's way easier to fix the company."

Elizabeth nodded in agreement. "Really, Jackson, you messed up bad with Natalie. If all of our fates are tied together with you successfully getting Natalie back, you should give the helm to Chris now."

Lori stepped forward and placed her hand on his arm. "Jackson, relationships are hard. When people don't turn out to be who you thought, working back from that is a beast. I think it's admirable, but maybe if you concentrated on saving Connected, you'd be able to do that, and it would be enough."

Jackson looked at the group standing in the hallway and had to take a deep breath. This was his family.

"I tell you this so you can take some time talk amongst yourselves and decide if you are going to work with me or not. Natalie and I will be running Connected with Gran's blessing. Now that you've all had your say and I've had mine, I've got to get ready for the party. Think about it," Jackson said as he walked through the crowd, and got into the open elevator to go home and change.

Six

She struggled between putting on a business suit or a party dress for tonight. The coffee incident had been the wake-up call she needed. Natalie was here to do a job. She was going to get dressed, call an uber, stay for the appropriate amount of time and then come home. She let out a breath and put on the green dress. It was a favorite of hers, but she hadn't really been anywhere that she could wear it.

When the bell rang, she took one look at herself and then got up. If Gina's dinner had arrived, it was time for her to leave.

"Got it," Gina called. A few moments later, Natalie was still fussing with whether to wear the necklace or not when Gina called. "Natalie, you've got a guest."

She opted not to put on the necklace and went out, to see him standing there.

"We meet again, Gina," he was saying as she came around the corner. "I came by to take Natalie to the party. I was hoping she'd hold my hand and protect me from the gang."

"Oh yes, Jackson Banner, you are indeed the full package." Gina chuckled. "Natalie is really good about defusing situations and bringing order."

"She always has been, amongst other great traits."

"I'd love to hear about the other traits."

"Gina, I'm here," Natalie said as she walked into the living room.

"I see we've summoned her from the bedroom," Gina said with a smile as she looked at Natalie. "You didn't tell me you were having a prince pick you up." As Gina walked by her, she leaned into Natalie's ear and whispered. "Or maybe I should say a king."

Natalie gave Gina a disapproving look. She should have known that Gina wouldn't pass up any opportunity to mess with her about Jackson. Gina and her were friends, but for the last couple of years, Gina was also the one who told her she needed to get out more and socialize.

Trying to forget Gina's teasing, she turned to focus on Jackson, and she was not prepared. Jackson was dressed in a black dinner jacket and a white shirt. His tousled hair made it seem like he had just left a party. His eyes took her in from head to toe, and then his mouth curved up in an appreciating smile.

"Beautiful as always." Jackson held out his hand. "Would you do me the honor?"

It was like time had stopped, and Natalie focused on Jackson's hand. What was she thinking, being here with Jackson? She should have told him to go away, that she could get herself to the party. Gina cleared her throat, and Natalie pulled herself together. She looked over her shoulder to see a smiling Gina.

"You won't need me," Natalia assured Jackson, "remember they're family."

"That's exactly why I need you." Natalie saw Jackson nod at Gina before opening the door. "I'll make sure to bring her back."

Gina laughed. "She can come back by uber, you know. I think she was planning on using it to go."

Jackson smiled. "That would make me the lowest of the low to not bring her home. Don't worry, I've got this."

Natalie looked at them both. "Hello? I'm here, and I want you to know I can make my own decisions. Let's see how the evening goes and then I'll make a decision."

Jackson gave her a grin. "It's that take-charge attitude and independence that I miss."

When she stepped outside and saw the black Mercedes-Benz, she looked back at Jackson. "You do know you're overdoing it. I can make it by myself, you know."

"This isn't about doubting what you can do. It's about me trying to make up for missing coffee. Besides, I was telling the truth when I said that I needed you tonight to face the horde."

He held open the door for her, and she looked up at him as she took her seat. "The great Jackson, afraid of his family?"

He closed the door and then got in behind the wheel. "For the record, I'm not afraid of them. I am not known for my gentle words or easy manner. Being surrounded by a group of people who think they can do my job better is not going to make me more sociable either."

"Yes, well, social graces were never your strong point." Natalie shook her head. "I'm sorry. It's not appropriate to bring up the past of any kind so—"

He tapped the steering wheel, and she looked up at him. "If we are going to make it working together, or whatever else may happen, we can't go around holding our tongues, afraid to speak the truth or accidentally going over old ground. So who do you think would gain the most from sabotaging our contracts at Connected?"

Natalie watched him pull out of the parking spot, turn on the music, and wait for her answer. "You have got to be kidding me."

"No, I figure I'd ask you. You have a before and after look that I don't. I know they've all called you by now, and I've finished looking at the books, so I know the problem with the domestic contracts are internal, not market-related."

"How do you do that?"

"Do what?"

"We were talking, and then out of nowhere you ask me which one of your family members do I suspect is betraying your family. Do you think there may be a problem here?"

"I do, and I'm trying to get your opinion. I want your input."

"My input is that you should trust your family. They have faults, but they're still your family. Also, get some help on your emotional intelligence."

"You know you aren't the first person to speak to me about my emotional intelligence. I read the book, you know."

Natalie put her hand to her head. "I can't believe we are having this conversation, but I shouldn't be surprised. Tell me, what's your plan on fixing this?"

"I was thinking I'd call an expert in the field to do the investigation quietly. While they are looking into it, I can mitigate the day to day issues."

Natalie folded her hands over her chest and looked out the window.

"Some things never change. You don't trust them. How could I think you would ever trust anyone else?"

The car pulled over, and she turned to see Jackson looking at her.

"It's not the best place, and it's certainly not what I planned, but there's an elephant in the room with us. I want to get rid of it now, or at least address it."

"Jackson—"

Jackson held his hands up and then brought them together as if he were about to pray.

"Nat, I messed up. A year ago—"

"Don't—"

"Please, Nat."

She wasn't sure she could do this. Be this close to Jackson and talk about what had happened. She knew this would have to be addressed, but she thought she had time. Looking at the intensity in Jackson's face, she knew that time was over.

She nodded for him to go on.

"A year ago, I offered you a box with a key to my place to move in with me. You thought we were going to get married. When you asked when was the marriage, I was scared, and I made a joke about it. I was wrong."

"Wrong Jackson? Wrong is when people lie. Wrong is when a person steals. You hurt me. I trusted you, and you hurt me. That is way more than wrong."

"Nat, there aren't words to tell you the terror that came over me when you said marriage. We had been together for two years, and I knew I kept you happy most of the time, but if we were married, you'd see me. You know the guy you just said needed some help with his emotional intelligence?"

Natalie shook her head. "That's not fair, Jackson. Don't try to put this on me."

"I'm not. I'm saying I know me. I didn't want you to get to know everything about me and leave. I have a talent for driving people away."

Natalie felt the tears run down her face and wiped them away.

"Jackson? Why didn't you trust that I would love you no matter what?"

He reached out and wiped an errant tear from her face. "Because it's never been done before."

He turned back to the road and started the car again. She let his words sink into her, and all of a sudden, the world became a way more complicated place. She thought she was here to get over Jackson. In a few short words, she wasn't so sure that was the goal anymore.

They pulled up in front of Sherry Banner's house. It was right out of a snow globe. A two-car garage, large front lawn, and lights along a path to the front door. When the car stopped, Natalie reached out and covered Jackson's hand on the wheel.

"First things first. Find out who is sabotaging the company, and don't be so quick to jump to conclusions."

"I've seen the books."

Natalie patted his hand on the wheel. "Don't let your distrust of people rob you of your family."

He looked at the door and then at Natalie. "Nat?"

"You didn't before, but trust me now. Don't be the unfeeling person they think you are."

"And you? You think that too?"

Natalie hesitated before giving her answer. "I'm reserving judgment."

Jackson sighed. "Well, I guess that's better than nothing. I still think this is a mistake. If Gran tells them she's supporting me, and they don't support me on the board, I'll strip them of their shares that were only given to them because I wanted them to feel as if they were part of the process. That decision made them think they could get rid of me as CEO."

"Figure out the problem, and it won't matter who supports who."

"You think I can do all that?"

"Sure hope so. Besides, they're your family," she said with a smile.

"Let's hope they remember that," he said.

"Of course they will, you'll see," Natalie said as they left the car and went inside.

Seven

"He's been gone so long, it's not like he's really family!" Chris growled as they walked into the room.

Jackson leaned over to Natalie's ear. "I don't think they are feeling family orientated now."

"Behave, Jackson," she whispered back to him. "Take the high road." She had to refocus her thoughts. Having Jackson whisper in her ear was like get a shock of electricity and not being able to shake it off, the tremors just ran through her body as she tried to keep her focus.

"You can't just strong-arm people into agreeing with you," Elizabeth declared outraged. "This is a family business, and we need to do the best thing for the family."

"You know I keep getting reminded that it's a family business more so than ever these days. Before I come back to all of this love and affection, I need to get something to wet my throat," Jackson said.

Natalie looked at Jackson as he grabbed a soda and poured it into a glass and then went to look out the window. The others stood on the other side of the room, looking like a bunch of vultures waiting to attack.

She thought back to when they were together. Had she missed this? How alone he was even in his family? Natalie saw Gran before anyone else as she came in and went to her right away.

"Hello, Gran."

"Hello, Natalie. I see the family is expressing their displeasure," she said as she took a seat.

Natalie was confused. "Aren't you going to stop them? He came back because we asked him."

Gran looked up at Natalie and gave her a look of regret.

"I can't step in here, Natalie. Jackson is a big boy. If I step in, then they'll think I run the company and not Jackson. He knew it would come to this. He's been in this position almost all of his life. He has to make tough decisions, and that responsibility doesn't breed friendships."

Disappointed, Natalie went to Jackson. As she approached him, she heard the complaints of the family members. They were like hyenas, nipping and picking at him with bits of history and petty problems. No matter what anyone thought, even Jackson needed someone to be on his side.

"You've been more like a consultant than a CEO. For you to be able to tell us what to do doesn't seem fair at all," Lori quipped.

Jackson didn't turn towards her when he answered. "Feel free to hire a consultant or a company to try and do what I do. They're going to ask for a percentage of the domestic business. Then you won't have to worry about me telling you what to do. You'll worry about an outsider trying to take the company."

"Don't make it seem like you're doing us a favor. You're probably here to run the company into the ground, and then your company can buy it," Chris spewed for all to hear.

Natalie made her way past the "family" and went to stand in front of Jackson.

"I'm ashamed I went to get him," she said in a terse tone. "Jackson is here to save Connected and the family business. Is it a shock that he wants your support?"

All of the Banner's turned on Natalie.

"For a consultant, you seem to have a lot do with what's going on," Lori said, "did you two make some kind of deal?"

Natalie looked Lori in the eye and stood to her full height to make Lori lookup.

"I didn't betray Gran's trust and cut a side deal. I'm shocked you think Jackson would have taken one."

"Maybe we have all been looking in the wrong place. It's always the innocent ones that show up out of nowhere that are a concern. So what is it? You couldn't get him to the altar a year ago so you cut a deal with him to neglect the company and then you two could sell it off for a tidy profit getting whatever you could?" Elizabeth asked as she eyed Natalie suspiciously.

Jackson's voice cut like a whip cracking in the air.

"Elizabeth, you are done asking Natalie questions. In fact, all of you are done asking Natalie questions. She was under some misguided impression that you all wouldn't bite the hand that's trying to save you, but she doesn't understand you like I do. Wild animals take a bite first, and then sniff for friendship last."

Howard spoke up. "Jackson, what are you trying to say?"

Jackson looked at every one of his relatives that were standing around him. "This is not a warning.

There will be no discussion. Natalie is mine. She takes orders from no one but me if at all. If somehow you forget that, I will forget that I'm here to help you and go back to my little company and never even look back. Are we all on the same page with this one?"

Everyone looked at one another. When no one said anything, they turned to Gran sitting on the couch.

"Oh? Now you all are looking at me? You want to know what I think now? I think that is one Grand way of staking a claim," Gran said as she laughed.

"All of the consultants have worked for Gran," Chris said. "She's had her hand on the pulse of things, and that's been the way."

"No, Chris, that was the way. Natalie works with me, and me alone. If anyone breaks that deal, I'm done. At this rate, Connected will be dead in the water in eighteen months' time."

No one spoke. Natalie could feel the eyes of the family on her. Even though she had just newly arrived as well, she could see the wheels of suspicion building in Lori's and Elizabeth's faces. A bell rang and broke the silence in the room.

"Well, that's the sign that dinner is ready," Gran said. She stood up and walked through the crowd to the doorway that led to the dining room. "Are you all done?"

Natalie took a deep breath and held her head high. She was about to take a step when she felt a hand on her upper arm. She looked to see Jackson. He smiled at her and then spoke to the room.

"I think we're done here for the night. I think it will be much easier for all of you to talk about me when I'm not here. And as it would happen, I owe Natalie some coffee. So while I make good on my promises, you all decide if you can agree to my terms. If not, let me know, and I'll have my items and Natalie's cleared out by ten in the morning."

No one said a thing, and Jackson guided her out of the house and to the car.

Never had she been so happy for Jackson to make a decision without consulting her. She wasn't sure how she would have made it through the evening, but she would have. After Jackson had laid down the law, she had expected the dinner to be filled with barely disguised snipes and dirty looks. She had been in the car for less than five minutes when she received a text from Chris.

"Well, that's different," she muttered.

"What's up?"

"Chris just texted me saying he'd like to talk to me alone when I get a chance."

"I bet he would," Jackson said sarcastically.

"Jackson?"

Jackson held up his hand. "Let me say that tonight was all that I expected from my family and more. No more talk about them. I was completely serious when I told them I plan on honoring my offer of coffee, but I can't just give you coffee after I took you away from dinner. So, do you still like Chinese?"

Natalie smiled and nodded.

Eight

"You know everyone thinks the best food places are in the city, but I actually prefer some places in Queens. There's no wait, and the food is amazing." Jackson said as he drove. They drove for about fifteen minutes, and then Jackson stopped on a block with a bunch of storefronts. He parked the car and looked at Natalie.

"Can you walk down steps in those shoes?"

Natalie was confused but nodded. Jackson got out of the car to open her door. He offered his hand to get her out.

"Your dinner awaits."

Natalie got out and looked around the poorly lit street. Jackson didn't seem to mind that his Benz was next to a stack of black garbage bags. They walked across the street, and as they got closer, Natalie saw a light. They walked three more feet, and then it was clear the light was coming from a stairway that went below ground. At the top of the steps was a sign that flickered and spelled, Momma Lee's.

He noticed her hesitation and gave her a smile.

"Come on, Natalie, I've got you."

She took a breath and followed him below. After she got past the steps, Natalie could see that inside was a cozy restaurant. There were about ten tables covered in red tablecloths. There were several ceiling fans going, and from the door, you could see straight into the kitchen. On the right was a desk that had a credit card machine, menus, and an old fashioned cash register. A small Chinese woman peeked around the register and called out.

"Jackson, my boy! It's been too long," the woman had perfect British tones.

"Momma, I'm sorry I've been busy."

"No worries. I see you have a lady friend. Have a seat at your table, and I will be right with you."

Jackson led the way. There were two other couples in the room, and they looked up and nodded at Jackson. Natalie watched him nod back and then go to the back table. She watched his body maneuver around the table with a grace that would be lethal in most men. She would have thought they'd look out of place. Instead, no one seemed to notice or care. When Jackson got to the table in the back, he pulled out a chair and then gestured for her to take a seat.

"After you," Jackson said, then stepped back and waited.

The gesture caught her off guard. It seemed in the past they were always eating in or going to a meeting, and moments like these were few and far between. When she hesitated, he came around and put his hand on the small of her back to guide her in.

His touch was enough to wake her up. "Thank you," she said as she took a seat. As he was walking back to his seat, she thought of his hand on her back. She couldn't remember being so aware of the warmth of man's hand, or the curve of his fingers. She knew he wasn't making a move on her, he was just making sure she was okay.

Moments later, a woman who she assumed was Momma Lee showed up with a smile.

"Do you have a favorite dish?" Natalie asked Jackson.

"Yes, everything on the menu," Momma Lee said. Now that she was closer to the table, Natalie could see that Momma Lee had slight crows feet around her almond-shaped eyes but had otherwise flawless skin. She guessed the woman to be in about her late sixties. She had a slim physique and a face that had very little makeup on and penciled-in eyebrows. Momma turned her gaze on Natalie and raised an eyebrow.

"So you're the woman who had him in a funk for the last year? Jackson has said only nice things about your intellect and your character. He didn't say how beautiful you were. I think that's a good sign from a man." She turned to Jackson. "You going to try and fix this?"

Jackson smiled and looked at Natalie. "I'm giving it my best shot."

"Good. Don't try, do. I'd hate to see you down in the dumps again. You two look good with one another. Not as good as me, and Mr. Lee did but good for your generation." She focused her attention on Natalie and once again raised a questioning eyebrow. "You want me to suggest something, or are you going to let him make all the decisions?"

Natalie picked up the paper menu that was on the table and quickly scanned it as Momma turned back to Jackson. "Coke?"

Jackson nodded.

Momma faced Natalie.

"Lemonade," Natalie responded.

"Jackson usually gets a number four, which is just lo mein and sesame chicken. I don't recommend it for you, too much starch. I have fresh fish, and I can give you a small bowl of brown rice. I think you should get that."

Natalie nodded and put her menu back in its place. Momma hadn't written a thing down, and Natalie didn't want to offend her by pointing it out. Momma gave her a look and smiled. "He's a fixer-upper, but he's a good man." With the order in her head, she walked away.

"That would be Momma," Jackson said when she left. "It's been a minute since I've been here with anyone and I'd forgotten how Momma could be so—"

"Forthright and transparent?"

Jackson smiled. "That is a way to say it.

Natalie smiled back. "No worries. I like her. She seems to say what needs to be said."

Jackson looked around. "This place has been here for years. She stayed here even after Mr. Lee passed. I met her when I graduated from college. One of my friends brought me here because it was one of the only places we could afford."

Momma came back and put the drinks on the table. She didn't say a word and Natalie marveled at how she showed as much discretion as any expansive restaurant where the wait staff was supposed to be unseen but efficient.

Natalie took a sip of her lemonade before speaking. "So, you didn't seem all that surprised by the party," she began.

"No, but I had hoped otherwise. If for no other reason than you thought it would be that way. However, I have a long history of the family wanting what they want from me, and anything else just isn't important."

"I know they were happy you came back, it's just the shock of you taking away their choices is a bit much."

"It was much when I asked for something, but it wasn't much when they needed it. Everyone knows that I have the same gift that my dad had when it comes to business. They want to use it, but they don't want it to cost anything."

Natalie winced. "That sounds a bit cold."

"It is what it is. This happens a lot in the city. People want what they want. When money gets involved, you find that even family can forget you're a person. I hoped it would be different. In fact, the only time that I've known it to be different has been with you."

Natalie gave him a long look. "It's odd how I thought we were so close. Now I find that I had bought into a lot of the image like everyone else. When we were together, it always went smooth. The first time I saw you, I thought, this guy has it all. He looks great, he's got money, and his family owns a successful company. His life is pretty rockin'."

Jackson twirled the fork on the table. "I hear that a lot. I should be so grateful for all that I have. I am grateful, and it's true I'm doing better than a lot of people. You know what, I'll tell them tomorrow. They don't have to support me as CEO; they can try to do whatever they want."

"I know it's not what you want to do. Waiting for them to support you doesn't seem like the smartest thing to you, but I think you should give them a choice. This is about what will happen to you all as a family," she said.

"Really? Why?"

"Because you're actually better than they are. You don't need to use their tactics. I know you can save the company, and they'll see you are the best man for the job."

Jackson raised his eyebrows. "It's a lot to put at risk."

"I agree, but it's about how you get it done as well, isn't it?"

Jackson stopped and looked at her for so long she started to get nervous under his gaze. This was the intense Jackson that she knew. The man who, with a look, could start the butterflies in her stomach. She wanted to reach up and make sure there was nothing on her face. Instead, she defaulted to the other option she had when she was nervous, babbling.

"I think the way it goes," she said quickly, "is if you want people to think you've changed or you want a different reaction from people, you've got to act differently. They've got to see the difference in you. It's not really fair because most of the time, you're showing that you can be a good person before they've shown they can be a decent person to you."

Jackson smiled and shrugged his shoulders. "I know you're right, but it just doesn't feel like it right now."

Natalie was taking a sip of lemonade, and she coughed as she swallowed too quickly. "You think I'm right?"

"What, you think I'm so set in my ways I can't see someone else's view?"

Natalie shrugged. "Let's just say that I haven't seen that softer side of you yet," she said with a smile.

The food appeared, and they both fell upon their dishes. After a couple of bites, Natalie looked up, embarrassed.

"It's really good."

Jackson waved her off. "Eat, I get it."

After they had finished eating, they both sat back, the dishes were moved, and the bill appeared. Momma Lee handed it to him.

"A woman is impressed when a man leaves a big tip. It shows he can take care of the necessities.," Momma Lee said.

"Thank you for reminding me."

Momma lee grinned and gave a bow to them both. "Jackson, don't stay away too long. You know you need to see the sun like everyone else. Too much work makes you grumpy."

She walked away, and Natalie leaned towards Jackson. "She gets to tell you about the tip?"

"She does. In this restaurant, Momma Lee is like my mother."

Jackson left a healthy tip.

"Thank you for dinner."

"Coffee?"

Natalie looked at her watch. "I'll take a rain check."

Jackson smiled. "Of course."

The drive back was silent. Jackson put on some slow jazz music, and the both of them were comfortable not talking. When he pulled up to her place, he parked in front of her house and then got out and opened the door. When she got out of the car, he closed the door behind her, and she looked at him and said, "Thank you, the food was good."

She started to go on about the evening, but before she could get the words together, he bent down and gave her a kiss on her cheek.

"Thank you, and I do plan on collecting on that coffee raincheck," he whispered, and then he stepped aside so she could go to her house. He stood there by his car until she was in the door. When her door was closed, she looked out the window and watched him drive away.

Her hand went to her cheek, and she had shivers that radiated down her back. She turned and placed her back against the door. Natalie wasn't the one to sugar coat things to herself. She was still attracted to Jackson. He almost seemed like a new man, or maybe one she didn't really know at all. She never thought she'd be this vulnerable to Jackson again, yet here she was. Her cheek still pulsing from a kiss that was so chaste it didn't even bear telling anyone about.

This new Jackson was dangerous. She had known this was going to be a fight, but now she wasn't sure what side she was on. She wouldn't jump to any conclusions like she did the last time. If she wanted to be cured of Jackson, either way, she was going to have to tread carefully if she didn't want to get hurt again.

Nine

"So Cinderella, how was the Prince last night? Was he a prince or a frog? I'm assuming due to the late hour you arrived home and the fact that Obi is still here that he must have been more prince."

Natalie walked into the kitchen to see a grinning Gina at the table. "It was a business party."

"Wow, talk about denial. What is going on with you and Jackson, Natalie?"

Natalie had been about to drink her coffee when she put the cup down. "Nothing is going on."

Gina raised an eyebrow. "You were supposed to go to a work party. You left it early, and Chris Banner came by thinking you had come home. Did you, by chance, go out on a date with Mr. Jackson Banner?"

"No," Natalie said resolutely. "We couldn't have gone on a date. At best, we're friends and co-workers. I'm helping him get the company together. It was a moment of relief we both needed from the family."

Gina looked at Natalie and took a sip from her coffee. "Hmm. That is so interesting."

"It's not interesting. It's not anything!"

"So last night, did he kiss you when he brought you home?" Gina asked.

Natalie rolled her eyes and threw her hands up in the air. "He did, and it didn't matter. He gave me a kiss on the cheek. It was simple, unassuming, and cute."

Gina laughed. "You sound disappointed."

Natalie opened her mouth and closed it, like a fish out of water. "Did you want me to wait a couple of more days before we say you like him?"

Natalie pushed the coffee cup aside and dropped her head into her hands. "No, we don't have to wait. I just don't know what's going to happen." When Natalie looked up from her hands, she saw a disgruntled Gina with her arms folded across her chest.

"Okay," Natalie whispered. "I do know that I'm going to give him a chance. That for this to be really over, I have to make sure I wasn't rushing, and I don't know. We have issues to discuss. I do like Jackson. I think I'm starting to get to know Jackson and not the person I wanted Jackson to be."

"Give a go, girl."

"Let's not read anymore into it than is necessary."

"You two look good together, but most important, he makes you live again."

Natalie looked at Gina. "I think I'm scared."

Gina reached out to her and patted her hand. "That's how you know you're going the right way."

Anything they were going to say was broken by the loud honking of a car. Gina went to look out of the window.

"Why am I not surprised that it's young, arrogant, and I think I'm ready for the world to be given to me, a.k.a Chris honking in his really expensive car?" Gina said. Natalie put her head on the kitchen table.

"When am I going to get a break?" Natalie moaned.

"He called last night, and he drove by. What does he want?"

"I don't know, but he said he wanted to talk to me."

"Oh well, if he said he wanted to talk to you and not Jackson or the matriarch, he is in deep trouble. Just go to his car and say no and be done with it."

"Gina, I'll hear him out," Natalie said, looking longingly at the coffee. Natalie walked to the door, grateful she had enough time to dress. Before she opened the door, Gina tapped her on the shoulder.

"Remember, if he's here, he's desperate," Gina warned.

Natalie opened the door, and there was Chris. He had on dark pants and a brown jacket with dark elbow pads on it. Natalie stepped back, and Chris stepped in. She watched him look around the room until he found Gina.

"Hello, Janet?"

"No, it's Gina."

If it was possible, Chris had found a way to annoy Gina even more.

"Ah, yes, I forgot. Hello, Gina."

"Hello Banner," she said and then went to sit at the table again. Just then, Obi came running out of the room. Chris took a step back.

"I didn't know you had a pet?" he said.

Natalie shook her head. "I'm just watching him. What can I do for you, Chris?"

Chris looked at Gina. "Gina, I need to talk to Natalie."

Gina looked over her shoulder "It's okay, you all talking won't bother me."

Natalie wanted to laugh at Gina's deliberate obtuseness.

"No, Gina, I wanted some privacy, it's a work issue."

Gina looked at him and then Natalie. She put on her best smile.

"Well, I suggest if you have something that important that you take Natalie on a drive or go to work because today is my day off. That means I have no intention of leaving this house if I don't have to."

It was obviously not the response he was expecting, but Natalie was expecting it so when Chris motioned for the door Natalie was already picking up her purse.

"I guess we're going for a drive," Chris said.

When the car started, Chris said nothing. Natalie thought about how different it was sitting in the car with Chris. This was a totally different experience than last night.

"Natalie, I want to thank you for talking with me today."

"I don't have a problem talking to anyone, Chris." As he continued to drive, Natalie thought she could feel the anticipation building in the car. Whatever it was, Natalie knew it was going to be big.

"Chris, it's not that I mind driving around with you, but can you tell me the issue?" Natalie asked. Chris had driven to a nearby park and then pulled in so they were looking at a small pond with ducks floating on top of it.

"I didn't think things would go the way they have. I mean, it didn't make any logical sense at all. If any shred of logic had been followed, then this wouldn't even be a question." Chris said as he faced her. She could see the pinch of his lips and the tensing of his jaw that told Natalie her first thoughts were right. Whatever this was, it was going to be something big and something unpleasant.

"You're not saying anything yet, Chris."

"Well, the short of it is I'm in trouble, Natalie. The kind of trouble that only Jackson could have caused."

Natalie really listened now. "Again, I need to know what we are talking about."

"What we're talking about is business. The international contracts were going so well. I knew that Gran was going to give me a chance with the domestic side. I extended some of my deals with my international people based on the domestic business I'd throw their way."

"How much business and did you sign a contract?" Natalie asked.

"I told them I'd send them about a quarter of a million dollars in business. There wasn't a need to sign a contract because my word is good enough for a lot of my deals until the paper comes."

"You did what?" Natalie said as her hand came up to her throat. If only she had pearls on, she'd be clutching them. "I'm not really familiar with Banner humor, but this would be a great time for you to tell me this was some sick joke."

Chris leaned back against the headrest and closed his eyes. "I can't because this is the truth." Chris hit the steering wheel and looked at Natalie with abject misery in his face.

"Well, you don't have a contract, go to them and tell them things have changed."

"Natalie, I can't tell them that. I don't think they would take well to that statement, and the other thing is my reputation would be wrecked if I told them I had to go back on my word."

Natalie groaned. "Chris, I can see how this is a bigger problem than the both of us."

"Listen, Natalie, it won't be so bad if you could just help me."

"Me?"

"If you work with me, then we can get rid of Jackson. I know I can run the domestic side."

"How am I supposed to do that?"

"I've been thinking, and I have a plan."

"I know I don't want to hear this," Natalie said.

"It's simple. You'll tell Gran that Jackson isn't fit and that he's probably here for revenge. She'll believe you."

"You want me to lie to your Grandmother?" Natalie said outraged. "I couldn't lie to her, in fact, that is exactly why we brought Jackson here so he could figure out what was wrong and tell her the truth about her operations."

"Natalie, it's not for you. You're going to be here today and then gone eventually. This is for the rest of us that have to find a way to live with Gran when you're gone. Let me have the opportunity to run Connected. I can do it."

"Well, if you are so sure you can do it, I suggest you go talk to your Grandmother."

Chris rolled his eyes. "You know I can't do that. Only the golden child, Jackson, can approach her."

"Then go talk to Jackson."

Chris stopped and gave her a long stare. "How can you think my idea is crazy and then say something like that? He doesn't respect me now. If I told him this, he would add it to his arsenal against me. Natalie, I need your help. Don't say no right away. Think about it. Okay?"

Ten

Jackson knocked on the door, trying to go over in his head how he would talk to Natalie. When the door opened, instead of Natalie like he expected, it was Gina holding Obi.

"Well, this house is a regular train station this morning. So what are you doing here on this fine morning Mr. Banner?"

"Regular station? Who else is here?"

Gina stepped to the side so Jackson could enter.

"So you're a little late because Chris already came by, and he left with Natalie."

"Chris?" he muttered. Jackson remembered the text Natalie received in his car, and his mind tried going through all of the information he'd gathered to find an explanation. Jackson started walking towards the door when Gina walked into his path.

"Not so quick. We need to have a talk."

Jackson hesitated and then looked around the house. "Is there something that you need in the house for you or Obi?"

Gina grinned. "I like that you're concerned about other people's and thing's welfare. It's going to make our conversation a lot easier."

Jackson let out a sigh and then resigned himself to sitting at the kitchen table. "Okay, I wasn't sure we needed to have a conversation, but let's do it. Maybe we can both help each other."

"Maybe?" Gina said. She put Obi down, who promptly went to his doggie bed without even acknowledging Jackson.

"Where did Chris take her? And what did you do to my dog?"

Gina counted the answers off on her fingers. "One, I don't know where they went. Last time I looked, Natalie was grown. Two, you get what you deserve when it comes to Obi. When you abandon your dog, he has to go on. You've had your say now sit down so I can get mine."

Jackson shook his head and stretched his legs out under the table. "Go for it."

"What are your intentions towards Natalie?"

Jackson stared at Gina for a moment and then laughed. "I think that Natalie is a little old to have her guardian have this conversation with me." He stood up as if he were going to leave.

"I disagree. I also think you should start to take me seriously. I know how you claim that you are going to woo her, but let me tell you I can make your wooing process an uphill climb. I just need to tell her after talking to you, I think you are a total nutjob and not worth getting back with. She will still make her own decision, but she'll take my opinion into account."

Jackson looked at Gina and wondered when women started running his life. He went back to the table.

"What exactly are you interested in?"

"I want to make sure you really want a relationship."

"I told her that," Jackson said.

"Do you know what that means for her?"

"I'm working on it."

"Well, let me give you a heads up she wants a man who doesn't mind being completely vulnerable with her. Do you think you can do that, Jackson? Because if you can't, I'm going to have to ask you to stay away from Natalie."

Jackson swore. "A man can care for a woman without baring his soul."

Gina smiled. "Of course he can, but you're special. You've already hurt her before, so now, baring your soul will be your 'I'm sorry.' Are we on the same page Jackson?"

"I hear you."

Jackson left and went to the office, he needed to find a way to save Connected, get the girl, and fend off avenging best friends.

"Thank you so much for coming," Gran said as Natalie walked into her house. "I want to thank you for indulging an old woman."

Natalie laughed. "I don't think there is anyone with enough guts to call you old, and it really is no problem to come to the house and do you a favor."

"Good," Gran said.

Natalie stepped into the house and guided Gran back to the living room.

"I'm expecting a delivery, and Jackson said it was important. I'm not going in today, so I decided to inconvenience you."

"Did he say why?"

"Nope, but that would be Jackson. He is always operating in a way that is totally his own," Gran said.

Natalie followed Gran into the living room, and they both sat down.

"I'm glad that we have this time to talk," Gran said.

"Is there something wrong?" Natalie asked.

"Wrong? No, I don't think there is anything wrong per se. I just wanted to go over my Grandson acting like a caveman and drawing the line saying you work for him."

"Jackson is adjusting to everything. I think he'll get better."

Gran nodded her head and smiled. "I realize the last time you were here, I never got a chance to show you anything. You and Jackson had such a whirlwind romance that I don't think I got to have any time with you. It was two years of meet, greet and falling in love."

They walked past the sitting room where the horde had gathered before dinner, and then walked down a hall. On the wall were pictures of a smiling Gran and a man. They walked past them all until they made it to what appeared to be a small library filled with as many pictures as books. There was a desk in the room, and it was cluttered with pictures as well.

"Have you ever seen my love, Rob?"

"No."

Gran picked up a picture, and again it was the smiling man who was in the photos in the hall. "He's a handsome man," Natalie said.

"Rob was everything to me. We loved as if every day was our last," Gran said wistfully. She continued to point to pictures and tell stories of how their love was, and then she got to a family picture where no one was smiling. Gran picked up the gilded frame and brought it to Natalie.

"This is Jackson and his parents."

Natalie wasn't sure what to say. The boy in the picture didn't smile. The man in the picture didn't look much better. The only one in the picture who looked as if they were going to take a picture was the woman. She had on a smile, but you could tell that while she was a beautiful woman, her smile didn't light up her eyes.

Natalie cleared her throat. "I had never seen a picture of his family."

"Oh come, come, you don't have to hold your tongue. They were a dreadful-looking family, and they were miserable in life. I'm not surprised you haven't seen a picture. I'm not even sure Jackson has one in his possession."

"Oh," Natalie murmured.

Gran took the picture with her and took a seat in a chair. "Please take a seat, Natalie. I'm not as young as I used to be and I look for every opportunity to take a seat."

Natalie smiled. "Gran, I've always been impressed with your stamina and your mind."

Gran smiled. "So what was I saying before I began basking in the glow of your compliments? Ah, yes, it's Jackson's family picture. I tell you it was almost Shakespearean in how tragic it was.

Jackson's father was a genius who was so involved in his gift of business that he had very little time for his wife. Jackson shared the same gift of business as his father, and again it was another way for them to share something and not include his wife."

Gran passed the picture. Natalie looked at the family

again and felt sorry for them, as they seemed even glummer, knowing the backstory.

"It must have been very hard on the wife," Natalie said.

"It might have been if she had been faithful, but she wasn't. She was accustomed to being the center of attention. Jackson's dad couldn't give that to her, so she found it in other places with other men."

"And his father never left her?" Natalie asked, thinking about her own past, and how her mother never left her father, who she knew wasn't faithful.

"His father had grown up around Rob and me. He was sure that love would win the day. He was sure that when it was all over, she would accept him and his gift. My son was such a dreamer. I might have been a contributor to that, as well. He only saw Rob and me, and I was beyond blessed to find the man of my dreams. We fought over the business and other things that married people do, but we never went to bed angry."

The bell rang, and Gran looked up at Natalie with a smile on her face and a watery gaze.

"The package is here. Can you get it and take it to Jackson for me?"

"Do you need help?"

"No, you go on. I'll be in here for a minute. If you could close the door when you leave."

Natalie nodded and then bent down and kissed Gran on the cheek. "Thank you for sharing."

Gran patted her on the hand. "I hope it helps. Now off with you before the boy leaves. The young are so impatient."

Natalie left thinking that maybe her own past was stopping her from having a love of a lifetime too.

Eleven

This was the first time Jackson was coming to the house at Natalie's request. It was late, so he wasn't certain if this was going to be a him and Gina date or what? How safe was she going to play them getting together? He heard her come into the office late this morning. He wanted to go next door and ask her what had happened between her and Chris, but he decided he'd wait for her to come to tell him. When she stuck her head in later that day, he was glad he waited. Then she shocked him by asking him to stop by.

He parked the car and then walked to her door. Just as he was about to knock on the door, Natalie opened it.

"Finally. You're here. Come in." Natalie took a step back and motioned him into the house.

She had pulled her thick, curly hair back into a bun, exposing the slender curve of her neck. The work clothes she had on earlier were gone and in their place were a tee-shirt and a worn pair of jeans. She looked so casually adorable that all he wanted to do was pull her close and bury his face against that exposed neck. There was some tension in her body though, that put him on alert. When he walked into the room, he wasn't sure what to expect, but when he heard Obi, he relaxed a bit and then turned to Natalie.

"Are you okay?" he asked.

"I'm good. I'm just trying to get it together. Ugh! Let's not look at me. Let's talk."

"I don't have any positive experiences associated with the phrase, 'let's talk' from a woman."

He sat on the couch and looked at her walking slowing to take a seat.

"Hey, I was joking. What's going on?"

He watched her sit next to him and clasp her hands in front of her. She pressed her lips together and then let out a breath. When he got ready to reach for her, she held up a hand.

"Please, Jackson. I need you to stay there, and I need to get through this moment first."

Jackson's whole body was tensing for action. He wasn't sure what was going on, but whatever had put Natalie in this state, he would fix it.

"Did someone hurt you, Nat?"

She let out a breath and gave him a sad smile. "No, I can't pin this on anybody but me. I'm physically okay. In the Grand scheme of things, I'm in the best shape ever." Again she closed her eyes and then clasped and unclasped her hands.

"I want to say something about us," Natalie said, looking at her hands.

"Okay."

"No, no, I can't start there," she said. She lifted her face and looked him in the eye and then gave a small cry of distress before looking away.

"We've never really talked about our childhoods and parents. Now I see that most things start there, and we both did a disservice to ignore that we were shaped by those moments."

"I didn't have a great childhood, and I didn't want to expose you to it."

Natalie looked up and gave him a sad smile. "But I think that's the point. It doesn't matter what it was. We can't help but expose the other person to it because it's a part of who we are.

"So here I go. My mom loved my dad. My dad was a bricklayer, and he was part of a union. So, my mom always said he was a good catch. A union man always had a job. Anyway, when he needed to move, we moved so he could make the most money. He was an attractive man, and he was always in demand. The ladies loved him, and he loved the attention as well."

Jackson sat back and felt a horrible moment of déjà vu. "He cheated on your mother," he said in a neutral tone.

Natalie nodded. "My mom said as long as he came back home, then she knew he loved her. He loved us. Then one day, he just didn't come home. We stayed as long as we could in the house. When the rent was a couple months past due, she moved us to a friend's house, and then she started dating. A couple of months later, she brought home my stepfather."

"And your father?" Jackson tried to keep his tone level. She didn't need to know that he understood how a parent could betray your trust. Oh, he had grown up and realized that his mother hadn't been mature enough or loved enough to stay with his dad, but there was a kid in him that raged against her.

"My mom told me never to mention his name. She told me that a woman needed a man to survive and that you couldn't look back, you could only look forward."

"I'm sorry," Jackson said, but it just seemed so paltry.

"I'm telling you this because I thought it was behind me, but I guess not. I'm also saying it because this is what has shaped what I want in a relationship."

Jackson stopped and looked at the tears that had tracked down her face. He didn't want to move or disturb what was happening between them.

"I want a relationship, Jackson. I want a man who isn't afraid to say he cares about me. I want a man who doesn't need to hide behind some macho mask and treat me like dirt. I want a man who won't mind that I ask for things in the relationship as well."

"I can see you've given it a lot of thought," he said.

"I've thought about a lot of things today, including us and our problem."

Jackson furrowed his brow. "What problem would that be?"

"We have a problem with trust Jackson. Neither one of us wants to risk anything, but we want someone we can trust unconditionally."

Jackson gave it some thought, and although he might not have put it together like that, Natalie's conclusion seemed accurate. Now that they had assessed the situation, what could be done? Was she going to ask for a contract? What would she request for trust?

"You can do this," she said in a low voice.

"Is that for you or me?"

Natalie looked at him with a bright smile. "It's for us both." She took a deep breath and let it out. "I want us to try to be open with each other and to give our relationship another go."

Jackson heard the words, and he wanted to jump for joy and step back at the same time. He knew more about her now than he did before. He knew how vulnerable she was right now, and at the end of the day, she would want him to be the same way. He was at the crossroads of saying yes to whatever she wanted, but there was a price, and he needed to make sure he was willing to do that.

"Do you understand what I'm asking Jackson?"

He looked at her, and the force of what she was asking him hit him hard. He stood up and ran his hands through his hair.

"I understand what you're asking. I—"

She stood up and placed her fingertips over his lips.

"Don't answer me now, Jackson. It took me a moment of reflection to get here. I want you to think about it as well. You know where to find me."

He nodded once and then turned to leave. When he was at the door, he felt like he should say something, but no words came to his lips.

She smiled at him as she held open the door.

"Think about it, Jackson. It's not a test, and there is no right or wrong answer."

He got into his car and looked at his steering wheel. He turned on the car and drove into the night.

Jackson didn't sleep well that night. He wasn't feeling any better by the time he arrived in his office and looked at the package that was dropped for him. He remembered Catherine saying Natalie had brought it over. When he opened the envelope, he wasn't sure which person he wanted to strangle more, Chris or Natalie.

He had to take a moment and think. He didn't know what Natalie knew or didn't. She had asked him if he could trust her. He had to know if he could give her what she wanted before he said yes.

He left his office and walked past Catherine into Natalie's office. She had made one wall into a screen, and she was looking at a proposal that had been submitted. The screen wasn't moving though, and she was waving a pencil in one hand on her desk. Her hair was up, but a couple of curly strands refused to be contained and they dangled down her neck. She had on a crème colored top on today and a dark suit. No matter how much she tried to look all business, there was a freshness about her that always seeped out.

"Nat?"

She jumped at his voice and turned to him, standing in the door. "What are you doing there, and why didn't Catherine announce you?"

"She didn't because I told her not to, and I have a simple question. What did Chris want with you?" He asked the question as he walked towards her. He found a wide-backed chair and took a seat. There were two wide-backed chairs in her office. They hadn't come with the office, so she must have personally picked them out. Natalie was good for that, making things homey.

"Is this your idea of trust," she said tightly. "You don't just go where you may or may not be invited and then start interrogating someone."

"Personally, I think I am showing a lot of trust by asking you what happened. I am not the enemy here. What did he want?"

Natalie crossed her arms over her chest. "He had a personal issue that he needed an opinion on."

Jackson looked at her and kept his mouth closed. It was clear to him that she would not be talking about Chris. Jackson wasn't in the best of moods and she needed him to very open to fix the Chris situation. There was no doubt he had to be told but she knew from experience when you told Jackson something could make all the difference.

"I just want to say that I'm trying this 'trust' as you call it, but it seems like I don't really understand how it works. I think we need some space from everyone here, and we need to jump into the problems of Connected. We're going to our Cali office this afternoon. Pack a bag for a couple of days."

She glared at him. "Wait a minute. I hope you don't think this is communication?"

He stood up. "I think it is. You see, I'm telling you why we are going. I'm providing separate beds. We do still have a company to fix, and I'll need your expertise and a fresh perspective when we meet with the business partners there."

She still had a skeptical look on her face, but she nodded. He didn't want to jump for joy because he knew she wouldn't appreciate it, but he had made some decisions, and it was time for him to show Natalie that he could be the man she was looking for.

Twelve

That man was a beast. He didn't know the first thing about trust or working together or respecting a person's right to privacy. Natalie knew this trip was some made-up thing because she didn't tell him about Chris.

That was the reason she was walking into the Monterey Plaza hotel next to the California offices of Connected Solutions that afternoon. The office was in scenic Monterey Bay. The area was clean, and the people were infinitely more open and much nicer than in New York. She remembered the first time she had come to Monterey with Jackson. That night she had called Jackson after the barking had started. She thought it was a band of free-roaming strays, but it had been the seals in the bay.

Today she was here as his second set of eyes if what he said on the plane could be believed. She used the spare office that Jackson kept here. He had gone to arrange some things, but he wanted her to get comfortable. The building itself was beautiful, like the area. Where possible, there were plants in the office, and frosted glasses served as a way for people to have privacy. There were no administrative assistants here as it was an open door, brainstorming facility. However, Natalie wished there had been one when she heard the steady clip-clopping of heels coming down the hall. This office was at the end of the hall so there could be no mistake about their destination.

Lori Banner stepped around the corner.

"Why is Jackson here, and just what are you planning?"

Natalie looked at Lori and thought the offices were *almost* perfect. Lori came into the office and took a seat in front of the desk. It was only the steady tapping of her shoes that gave any indication that she wasn't as cool and collected as she normally was.

As usual, Lori was dressed for the runway. She was in a red suit that clung to her just as it was supposed to. Her hair swayed free, and she had that model professional look.

"I'm here as a second pair of eyes only." Natalie took a seat behind the desk. If she had to face the Banner's today, she was going to do it as much as she could on her terms. "You see, Lori, in some ways, we are both in the same position. We have all agreed to do whatever it is Jackson thinks is best to save Connected."

Natalie equated listening to Lori tapping her shoes as modern-day water torcher. When Natalie still hadn't moved, Lori leaned forward on the desk.

"I think you know more than what you're saying."

Natalie thought of the things that Jackson had told her. Jackson was looking into every family member to make sure they were all innocent. He had already declared she was his and his alone. She had to honor the trust he had put in her by even telling her what his suspicions were.

"Listen, no one can know Jackson's mind until he is ready," Natalie said. "Right now, we are all doing the same thing, waiting on Jackson."

"He's been going everywhere and talking to everyone. These are not the movements of a person that is unsure," Lori accused Natalie. "He's with you the most now. He may have said you answer to him, but Gran writes all the checks, and we need to know what is going on."

"I heard you, Lori. Also, I'm well aware of who pays me. In that vein, we all need to be aware of what you brought Jackson home for. It was to save the company, and as far as I can tell, he is trying to do that."

"You know, Dad says there's too much trauma in his childhood for us to be able to completely trust him. I may not have a degree in any social science, but I agree, Jackson isn't someone to trust." Lori looked past Natalie to the large windows that showcased the bay. "He's so unpredictable."

Clearing her throat, she looked at Lori and tried to put on a comforting smile. "Jackson has a way of upending everything. I don't have anything to tell you, except that you all called him back. The best we can hope for is that he delivers." Natalie looked at her watch. "I'm sorry, I can't stay. I wasn't expecting you so I booked another meeting for this time slot."

"Natalie, please." Lori stood up and rubbed her forearms as if she were warming up for something. "I hope my family can count on you to let us know if Jackson does something drastic."

Natalie looked at Lori, and she could see there appeared to be real concern in her gaze.

"I'll make sure to let Sherry know," she conceded. "The relationship between her and myself would demand nothing less. As for the rest of you, I'm just a hired hand, and I can't see how you would equate that with me sharing any information with you?"

Lori's eyes narrowed, and her posture became stiff. "Just what is that supposed to mean?"

"It's not a matter of what is it supposed to mean. It's a matter of fact and truth. Sherry has always gone that extra step to help me out. I won't forget that, and of course, I would return the favor."

"Certainly, you're not going to be so petty?!" Lori hissed. "The whole song and dance about being loyal to Sherry but not the rest of the family is just a cover. Admit it, you've never forgiven me for not telling you what Jackson had in that box that day? This loyalty to Gran is just a screen and a poor screen at that."

"This has nothing to do with that day or the box."

"Sure, it doesn't." Loris stood up and went to the large window. Natalie wondered if she practiced what would be the best angle to stand at to look distressed. "Really, Natalie, I did you a favor by not telling you. You see how Jackson is now. If you had married him, then you'd be under his control like we are."

Natalie looked at Lori and wondered if she really thought she had done her a favor. "I can see how you might think that."

"Jackson only looks out for Jackson."

"Yes, he's focused."

"Besides, if I had told you about Jackson, he might have fired me. Me?!" Lori said, incredulously.

"Looking back in retrospect, you might be right." Nice to know she was concerned about us both, thought

Natalie. "Well, that is over. You don't have to worry about that because Jackson isn't here for you now. He's just looking to save the company."

"Is that all he's doing? I wonder."

Natalie paused, and the sneaky thought crept into her mind that maybe Lori could be the one. Natalie wasn't naïve. She understood people had all types of motivations, but she couldn't believe it was a family member.

"Lori, Jackson is here to save the company and to save the family."

Lori turned around, and for a moment, Natalie thought one of those perfect well-rehearsed tears were going to strategically fall down Lori's cheek, miraculously not messing up any makeup.

"Natalie, I think you don't really see him. He hasn't changed. He was out for himself before, and he's out for himself now. Time doesn't change a rotten apple."

Natalie and Lori jumped when they heard the clapping at the door. Jackson stood there, leaning in the doorway.

"I was so tempted to stay here as you itemized my flaws, but as it stands, you called me back because you couldn't handle the business. I need someone with a little more morality than me, so if you'll excuse us, I need Natalie in a meeting."

"Of course, Jackson. Let me get my notepad." Natalie gave a wan smile to Lorie and then followed Jackson out of the office.

As they walked into the elevator, Jackson started the question she didn't really want to answer. "I only heard part of the conversation, but did we recount all of the things I've done wrong or just this week's list?"

"Just when we broke up."

"Great, just what I need a reminder of bad times."

"Well, she felt like you might hold a grudge. You know you don't talk a lot to anyone and—"

"I think we should not talk about my inability to express my feelings right now. I have to say when I hear you retell some events, it makes me think you all think I took business from the Grinch."

Natalie looked down so Jackson wouldn't see the smile that had broken out with his comment. "That's a valid fact and just so you know. That was a very open comment."

Thirteen

This date was feeling more and more like a bad idea. She had accepted it on a whim during the meeting earlier and it was too late to cancel it. Rob had been in the meeting, and as soon as he had smiled at her, Jackson's mood had soured, and his glare had become oppressive. Lori's words came back to her, so when Rob had asked if she had plans for the night, she had given him a wide smile and said no, she didn't have any plans.

As the meeting came to a close, Jackson waited until the rest of the board had left.

"Dinner plans?" he asked in a flat tone.

"Yes, Rob asked me."

"I thought we'd do dinner."

"Do we have more business to discuss?" Natalie asked.

Jackson looked up and shrugged his shoulders before answering. "I guess not, have a good time."

All evening she had been pondering her curt answer and trying not to feel bad. This dinner didn't seem fair to Rob or Jackson. She had already resolved to make it short but polite.

After Rob and she were seated, he wasted no time talking about the topic he really wanted to discuss.

"I don't get Jackson," Rob said.

Natalie sighed. Wow, he wasn't even going to wait until after the meal to begin pumping her for information. She was kind of glad that he had an ulterior motive for the dinner. It didn't make her feel as bad for scheduling it just to get at Jackson.

This was a common theme. Everyone thought she had some secret insight into Jackson. All of them had been disappointed to discover she was waiting in the wings for his moves just as much as they were.

The other thing that turned this dinner into more bitter than sweet was that Rob had been one of the few people who was there for the debacle before. When he had come to her office when she'd just arrived, she thought he was the welcoming committee. Now she realized that he was just like everyone else.

Rob was concerned about his job. With the company losing projects, his job as a project manager was on the line if this didn't get fixed. While her heart was sympathetic, her moral compass was clean. Until Jackson figured it out, there may be leaks, but it wouldn't be her.

"Who can know what goes on in Jackson's mind?" Natalie asked and then tried to pretend interest in the rather bland hotel menu. In the grand theme of things, the only thing she'd want to order from the hotel restaurant was a burger and a sandwich. Everything else was taking a risk that was as profitable as playing Russian roulette.

"Certainly he's given you some hint?"

"Nope."

Rob reached out and pulled her menu down so he could see her face.

"I expected better from you, Natalie. We've been working side by side. You know the Banners can be ruthless. I'm thinking if we can stick together, then we can survive and finally take more than the scraps that they choose to give out. I know you just came back to the game, but you should remember that the Banners look out for themselves."

Natalie's appetite was gone. She was thinking that maybe it was time to order a salad and call it a night.

"I don't have anything to share, Rob. There's nothing that I can say at this point. Jackson is doing what he normally does, he works alone and then tells everyone what he's found and decided. He's reviewed all of the projects of the last six months. When he finishes, then he'll discuss it with me."

"I don't know what the problem is. Everyone knows that business is just drying up on the domestic side. Connected has been in the business for a while, but they haven't been able to keep up. They need new leadership, and the old lady will only consider her family."

"I don't know if that's the only option, but we'll all have to wait no matter what."

"Banners think because they have been at the head of the pack that they know how to stay. Times change, and they should be open to new blood. They don't understand that not changing, is dying."

"Connected has had ups and downs before and never needed to do anything more than hold on."

"Those were old techniques." Rob picked up a bread roll and pulled it apart. "They need new attempts. If they aren't going to change their process, then they're going to lose it all."

"I think that Jackson knows what he's doing. He'll make the hard decision if he needs to," Natalie said evenly. "He'll get it done."

Rob gave her a long look. "You speak like the rest of them. Jackson isn't the next savior."

"Jackson isn't going to win any awards for personality, but there's no one else I'd trust to save a business from going down."

"You mean you're placing your bets on the thoroughbred?"

Natalie smiled. "I would have never quantified him as that, but I guess you're right."

Rob gave a wan smile as he dipped his bread in the bowl of olive oil on the table. "Natalie, I want to make sure I can count on you. You know we are both in the same place trying to do the same things. We're getting older, and we both need to watch out for our careers. Just keep a co-worker on the up so I can move appropriately."

"I hear you, Rob, and I'll do what I can," she said flatly. "I think I'd like a salad instead of a whole meal."

She could see he wanted to keep pumping her for information—or assurances, she wasn't sure which—but it didn't matter, she was done. The moment he decided not to push, she could tell. His face changed, and he had a smile on him that seemed easy going.

"Like a woman, I invite you to dinner, and you want plants. No problem. I hear the chef is from one of those healthy spas. Talking about other members of the family. I saw Lori around here."

"Lori, you mean back in New York?"

"No, I mean here. She's been too busy handling business to think about how the business is going."

Natalie thought of how aggressive Lori seemed today and how she hoped that Lori wasn't the person Jackson was looking for.

"What makes you think Lori is occupied?"

"She's been wining and dining one of the international customers," Rob said as he looked over the drinks menu. "Maybe she's going to take over from her brother." He laughed. "The old woman may not want new blood, but they all know the international business is where it's at."

Natalie tried to think of a reason why it would be so, but nothing came to mind. "Maybe Lori was meeting a contact with Chris, and he needed translation?"

Rob waved down a waitress. "No, I don't think so. It was Chris's contact. I was leaving the corporate building, and the contact Marvin Scott, was waiting for her in a limo outside of corporate headquarters. Marvin is bi-lingual as well."

Natalie tried to find a way to defend Lori. "There must have been another reason."

"I think you put the Banners on too high of a pedestal. At the end of the day, each one of them wants it all. Now that the old lady is getting old, there's blood in the water, and everyone can smell the opportunity. That's why I said what I said earlier."

"What was that exactly?" Natalie wanted to get back to her room and find out if what he was saying was correct. It would be an easy thing for Catherine to look up. The travel files would be an easy access item.

"It doesn't matter, really. Since I know I can count on you, it'll all be better now," Rob said with a large smile.

"We outsiders have to stick together. Right?"

"Well, I think you're right. We definitely have to do something," she murmured. Then Natalie looked around. "Now, where is that salad?"

She was never so happy for a dinner to end. For a moment, Rob had been looking at her like he might ask to have a nightcap. It would have been awkward, but she tried to stave off any thoughts he may have had by offering him a very cordial handshake in the lobby. What was even more disconcerting was that she wasn't sure how far Rob would go for them to "stick together."

If nothing else, it surely helped her see how everyone else saw her, Jackson's blind sidekick. While she may not be as blind as they all thought she was, Natalie knew her feelings were involved. She hoped the man she was getting to know was also discovering something about his feelings as well.

When she walked through her hotel room door, it led into a small hallway. A few feet in, it opened up to the right into the kitchen that had a small island. Further ahead, if she turned on the lights, she assumed she'd see the small couch and television. There wasn't a point in turning on the light. She was just going to go to bed anyway.

Jackson, she thought as she leaned on the marble island. Was she really thinking about Jackson? He was bold. He was unstoppable when he wanted something, passionate about what he believed in. Most importantly though, he had the power to hurt her beyond measure again or make a dream come true.

Who was she kidding? She wasn't going to bed with Jackson on her mind. She could watch a television show and maybe fall asleep in an hour. She reached for the light and jumped because sitting on the couch, was Jackson.

Natalie covered her mouth from shock as she looked at Jackson on the couch. Her hand went to her chest next, trying to still her thumping heart.

"I'm here because I wasn't sure how persistent Rob was going to be, but it wouldn't be real." Jackson's voice cut through the silence and wrapped around her.

Natalie took a couple of deep breaths and then leaned against the wall to pull herself together. It took all of three seconds for her feelings to go from shock to fury. Jackson was sitting on the sofa with his arms out, and his legs crossed. He didn't look harried or rushed, and all Natalie could think of was how long he had been there. As if he had prepared for the night, he was dressed all in black. He had a plastic bottle of soda in his hand, and he took a drink from it.

"So how long have you been here being creepy?" Natalie pushed off of the wall and walked closer to him, ready to give him a piece of her mind, now that she was thinking. Her hands were on her hips, and she was more than ready to deal with Jackson. "Jackson, what are you doing here?"

"I'm here to talk about my feelings. Isn't that what you wanted?"

"Now?"

"Did you go to dinner with Rob to make me jealous?"

The wind left her, and all of her fury was gone.

"How could you ask me such a question, and how would I know that would make you jealous?"

He tilted his head to the side, and then he took another drink from his soda.

"You came here with me, and then you were going

out with Rob. It's been a strategy that women have used for all time, and it's been used on me more than once."

"I'm sorry. I suppose women do use that as a tactic, but not me." This was Jackson and her. A moment ago she had been ready to give him a piece of her mind, and now she was willing to give him comfort for the pain and distrust he had been taught.

"Women use it, and I've been jealous before," he said quietly. "I was jealous tonight. You know what I really dislike about being jealous? It shows how insecure I am."

"Jackson—"

"Jealousy makes you lose control and puts you at the whim of another person."

Natalie walked over to the couch and sat next to Jackson. She reached out to him and wrapped her hand in his free hand as he spoke.

"You know it's an odd thing to think you can run a company, you can make millions, but another person can somehow take away all of your power and accomplishments by flaunting their preference of another person or even worse, making it seem like you have no place in their lives."

"A person who does that doesn't care about you because they don't know how to care about themselves yet."

"Maybe, but when you're very beautiful—"

"There are lots of beautiful people who don't do that. If someone is attractive and they do that to someone they are with, it usually means they're insecure too. Maybe that's not a fair statement because I don't know the details, but I know you were hurt, and it makes the actions cruel."

"Maybe you're right."

"Jackson, I'd never play that game with you. I went out because I was angry, and I thought you were being high handed, but I didn't think that you would be jealous over it."

"It doesn't give you a thrill to know I want to be with you that much?"

"No, and it would still be cruel even if I did it."

He took another long sip from his soda bottle and emptied it. "You're right. It's mean, and I want you to know I'd never do that to you either. No jealousy."

Natalie smiled. "So glad we can be in a debate about our relationship but agree not to make anyone jealous."

Jackson stood up and looked down at Natalie. The movement made her have to look at him from head to toe. He looked dangerous in black. His jeans were melded to his thighs, and his shirt was open at the top just enough to give a peek of the well-muscled chest below.

Why did this man have to be the one who had that effect on her? "Are we done, Jackson? I'm safe in my room."

"I know you had dinner." He held out his hand to pull Natalie close to him. "Coffee always seems to go poorly for us. Would you like to get dessert?"

"Now?"

"Yes, now. I think I need to de-stress after all that emotional sharing."

Natalie was standing in front of him so close she could reach out and touch him, but she didn't dare. There was a wave of heat and power that wafted off of Jackson. She had to remember to breathe, and when she did, it fanned the feeling between them. This was what it was to stand close to the heat and try not to get consumed.

"Dessert? At a place?"

"This isn't a trick. I'll take you somewhere. I'd like to go, and we'll have dessert. We can talk and do that sharing thing you like to do."

The longer he talked, the more his voice wrapped around her will. She lifted her eyes to meet his, and then it was decided.

"Yes," she whispered. "I would love to have dessert."

Fourteen

"You have got to be kidding," Natalie said.

"We need to get inside and get a seat," Jackson said, as he opened the door.

She looked around and decided to go with it. She wasn't sure where she had expected Jackson to take her, but what she never expected was for him to take her to a Rolling Donuts franchise site. The neon light on the outside of the store said they had the best ice cream and donuts within a 20-mile radius. Natalie wasn't so sure how impressive a statement that was considering it was in the middle of nowhere.

As he led her in the store and found a booth, she got nervous, and the butterflies were causing her to feel anticipation and dread all at the same time. She couldn't imagine why this would be the queasy moment. They were out in public, and in a franchise site no less. It was funny how, when she got what she was looking for, she either wanted more or she was scared that she got her initial request.

When asked what kind of ice cream she liked, she told him to decide. When he came back, he gave her what looked like a kiddie scoop of chocolate chip cookie dough with sprinkles. She took the cup and then sighed. Okay, she had to admit it to herself if no one else, that this sharing and discovering Jackson wasn't as easy as she thought it would be. When she didn't dig into her ice cream, Jackson noticed.

"You don't like chocolate chip cookie dough?"

She looked at her cup. "It's not the ice cream."

"You want a larger portion? I'm okay with that. I like women who eat."

She laughed. "No, that's not it either. I'm sitting here thinking this should be all romantic, and it's not the way I imagined it."

Jackson smiled. "So, you've been imagining things with me?"

Natalie rolled her eyes. "I have been imagining romantic meetings forever. Now I'm putting a face in the dreams."

"I know, it seems like there's a high bar, and I just got here."

Natalie jabbed her ice cream and took a bite. "It's not high; it's the rule."

"The rule now?" Jackson said, bobbing his head.

She rolled her eyes. "It's not the rule but the definition."

"Ahh, so why don't we do this: because I know you have an image in your mind on what should be happening, I'll let you go first."

Natalie pointed her spoon at him and waved it. "Are you serious?"

"Yes, go ahead."

Natalie smiled and put her spoon down.

"Okay, well first off, we would not be here. We'd be in a restaurant with romantic lighting,"

Jackson nodded. "You mean those expensive places they turn the lights down so you can't see your food?"

She closed her eyes and counted to three. "No, it's one of those restaurants that turn down the lights, so you think it's only you two in the restaurant."

"Ah-ha, go on."

"Then, when we're there, you would order a dessert that we would both share, and that has a lot of chocolate in it topped off with fresh sweet cream."

"I can see how the ice cream could be a little bland compared to that," he said in a gentle voice.

Natalie was looking into the ice cream cup and then continued on.

"Next, after a couple of moments of sharing the dessert, then we look into each other's eyes, and then you say 'I care about you, and I'm glad I met you.'"

He looked at her and nodded his head. "It's not bad. Maybe not mine, but I can see that."

Natalie looked at him, skeptically. "Okay, I've told you mine."

Jackson looked side to side and then pointed at himself. "Me? You want me to go? I thought I made my evening confession already."

Natalie folded her arms over her chest and waited.

"Okay, here are my thoughts, maybe not as clear as yours, but here goes."

He pushed his cup to the side, and reached out to touched her hand. He cradled her hands in his and smiled at her.

"Ooh your hands are cold, but I'm going to do my best and help you out anyway," he said with a laugh.

"I'll keep my hands to myself, thank you," said Natalie, as she pulled her hand back.

"I was trying to get you in the mood," He laughed. "Well, first, I'd bring you to an ice cream shop."

"Really," she said with a smile. "Why is that?"

"What you see around here is me. I don't like to go to expensive restaurants. I won't be whispering in a little French place, and I don't want to take anyone there because that's not me. This night would be perfect if I had Obi, and we all went out in a truck with a tub of ice cream. I'd open up the tailgate and lay out a blanket, and then we'd sit in the truck and eat ice cream and then talk about our hopes and dreams."

Natalie looked at him and then shook her head. "I think that is very you, Jackson."

"I try to be very transparent. We either get along, or we don't."

"So we're not going to meet on what's romantic. Why don't you tell me what you like about me?"

Jackson cocked his head to the side. "You're honest and faithful," he said. "I'm sure I've said it before, but everyone knows where they stand with you. You take people for the way they are. You may not agree with everything a person does, but it doesn't mean that you judge them or ostracize them. At the end of the day, the most important thing is, I like you as a human being."

Natalie smiled. "I like you as a human being to Jackson."

Jackson grinned. "Well, we've won half the battle. The rest is bound to come." He looked down at his watch. "Okay, Cinderella, it's time to go home."

He held out his hand and pulled her to her feet. The momentum pulled her into his arms.

"I've got you."

Natalie nodded and tried to remember to breathe in his arms. His arms were warm bands of security. Tingles roamed down her spine, and a slow heat wound through the lower half of her body.

"Don't look so scared. We're in the middle of an ice cream shop what can happen?" When he spoke, his breath brushed across her cheek and he smiled, but that smile did little to reassure her. She was now up close and personal with that black shirt. His shoulders were so much broader than she had thought before. Everywhere they touched were patches of heat seeping into her body.

"I'm not scared," she whispered.

She felt him shifting and knew at any moment he would lean down and kiss her. Instead, she felt his breath on her ear.

"You may not be scared, but I am. It's time to go."

Natalie didn't know what fazed her more, that she wanted him to kiss her or that he said he was scared. She didn't resist him when he started walking to the front door. She was right behind him, and they said nothing as they walked in silence.

Natalie looked at their hands and noticed how long his fingers were. She could feel the rough pads on his palms that spoke of long hours of work. His hands dwarfed hers and made her feel safe and secure as he engulfed her. It wasn't the romantic dream she had thought she wanted, but she was feeling great by the time they got back in the car. With jazz music playing in the car, and both of them riding on a high of just being in each other's company, Natalie had to rethink what she considered to be romantic.

Here she was in the car with a guy who took the long way to her hotel and had jazz music on and she was thinking about what a romantic night it was. When did her vision get kidnapped and replaced with this? She may not have known when it happened, but there could be no denying that she was feeling relaxed.

As the car rocked back to and fro, she felt all of her inhibitions fade away. She was thinking this was the way she had always imagined it. As the music settled over her, and Jackson's hand clasped hers, she felt herself drifting off to sleep. She was exhausted from all of the back and forth. She just wanted to relax and enjoy the moment.

"Natalie?"

"Yes?"

"We didn't talk about Chris and what he wanted from you?"

She heard the request, and she had almost forgotten about poor Chris. "Poor boy is in trouble, not sure if he needs a lawyer or a loan," she ended with a chuckle.

"How much money?"

Fifteen

Jackson's words were like cold water on her languid mood. Jackson talking about money became business, Jackson. She wasn't sure what was the best course of action: trying to play sleeping, or trying to clean up her statement by laughing it off. When she looked over at Jackson, both of his hands were on the wheel, and she could see the white of his knuckles. "I don't have an exact figure?"

"Ballpark it," he gritted out.

"Jackson, I really don't know, maybe a couple of hundred thousand," she murmured.

Jackson pulled the car over to the side and parked. Natalie closed her eyes and took a breath.

"Since this evening is about sharing our feelings. I want you to tell me why I shouldn't share my feelings and get rid of Chris tonight?"

Natalie had underestimated Jackson's reaction to the whole situation.

"Jackson, calm down and let's talk about it."

"It seems like there has already been a lot of talking. I think what's appropriate now is a lot of doing."

"We don't want to do anything we might regret," she said, trying to placate him.

"Chris has already done something he's going to regret, so let's just check that one off of the to-do list. How could he do that? How did he think you were going to get this money?"

Natalie looked at the maelstrom that was now Jackson and decided that right now, Jackson was a lot like a hot piece of steel that was in the fire. Maybe if she threw everything at him, they could get past this moment and move on to the cooling phase.

"He had a plan."

"Oh, I just bet he did. Who did he want you to go to for this plan?"

"Actually, the plan was to convince Gran that he was better suited to running the company."

Jackson leaned his head back in his seat and then started to breathe a little more evenly. Natalie thought the dangerous part was over until he spoke.

"Well, I have to give him credit about thinking he could run Connected. The problem isn't the ambition. The problem is he was going to use you to get there."

Natalie sighed. She couldn't even say anything to defend Chris. As usual, when it came to business, Jackson had an immediate handle on what was going on and why.

"The question, though, is why does he need it now?" Jackson said, turning towards her.

Natalie closed her eyes. "He thought Gran would turn to him to run the company, so he made some deals with his international contacts based on the idea he would be able to give them business. Now it's apparent he's not going to be assigned the CEO position. They want their money back."

"Hmm, it sounds like he was dealing with Marvin?"

Natalie looked at him, surprised. "I think so."

She watched him tap his fingers on the steering wheel and then murmur to himself. "Wonder if you were the first person he went to. If he knew the outcome wasn't sure that he'd get the helm when Gran called me, why didn't he go to Gran?"

"How could he go to her? He has been doing things to try and impress her that he's ready for more responsibility. If he goes to her with this, that will be totally gone."

Jackson's face hardened. "Well, there are several mistakes here. The first one was him going to you."

"He thought I was—"

"No Natalie. If he wants to play with the grownups, he has to fix his own problems, not pawn them off on someone else."

"Jackson, he's young, and he wants to be—"

"Yes, he wants to grow up and rule the world. So what were you going to do to help this young Caesar ascend the throne?"

"Well, I had some thoughts on the matter."

Rolling his hand, he pressed her for an answer. "What thoughts did you have? Put this at Gran's feet? Go to Marvin and tell him, sorry? What were your thoughts?"

Natalie's patience was wearing thin, and she tried not to obviously roll her eyes at Jackson's absurd suggestions.

"Stop jumping off the cliff already. I wasn't going to go to Gran."

"Why not?"

"I think it's important for Gran and Chris to talk to each other."

"I can't believe that even now you're looking out for their emotional health," Jackson said. "It's true, she's been very kind regarding references and the sort. Okay, you weren't going to ask her, what was the plan? I can't imagine you just leaving him out to dry, although that is what he deserves."

Natalie was trapped. This was not the way she wanted to lead up to this topic or the resolution that she had. She'd been mulling it over since she'd spoken to Lori.

The time for planning was over; it was now or never.

"I really thought I would let you address this problem as part of you resolving what appears to be a pretty consistent issue you have."

He looked at her and tilted his head to the side. "I'm sorry, I couldn't have understood you. I think you just said that you were going to give me this issue to solve because I was somehow a contributor to not only the problem, but to another problem related to it as well?"

Natalie smiled. "I'm so glad you agree."

"I didn't say I agreed with anything!"

"But, you articulated the problem so well!"

"Yes, I repeated what you said, but that doesn't mean I agree. What problem do you think I have that is relevant to Chris?"

"Personnel. There is a lot of uncertainty in personnel, and there doesn't seem to be consistent supervision of your staff, so they feel secure in their jobs when you walk away."

Jackson started to look out the window and in the back seat.

"Jackson, what are you doing?"

"I'm looking for the Director of HR because she said something close."

Natalie smiled. "So you should feel reassured that the both of us have found this shortcoming in you. Now we can work on it."

"Just hold on. I didn't' say I'm taking responsibility for Chris or the staff. We all get up in the morning and put our pants on the same way," Jackson said through clenched teeth. "I can't put a word in their mouths or heads when they wake, and I can't plan their lives. I give a wage for a task."

"I know you think you don't, but you do. It's all about expectations. When staff is given clear guidance and job descriptions, they until what their promotion path looks like. Obviously, this wasn't done with senior management, and as a result, you have Chris, voila."

Jackson looked around him and then put the car back on the road. Natalie thought this was the beginning of Jackson's understanding.

"Nat, this is what I'd do for Chris. Let him sweat it out. Gran will catch him, and then it will resolve itself."

Natalie peeked at him driving and saw his knuckles were no longer white. His shoulders seemed relaxed. "Okay, you can see that this is the right way, you just don't like it."

"Don't like it? I'd like to tell Chris the penalty for pushing others to do his work."

"I think you are taking this a bit far. He was desperate."

"It's not far enough at all, and when a man decides he wants to make those moves, he doesn't do it hiding behind someone else. More importantly, I don't like the way he thinks it's okay to use you to solve his problems."

Natalie didn't say anything. What could she say? *No, please don't care for me?* Fortunately, he pulled up in front of the hotel, and Natalie had the keys in her hand. She pushed the door open and then looked at him still brooding. He looked at her before she got out of the car. Natalie reached back and placed her hand on his upper arm.

"Jackson he made a mistake. You were young once too. He's looking for a way to prove himself."

"He's proved just why no one will trust him. You can't trade what you don't have. You're right; he made a mistake, and it needs to be addressed."

"So, you'll help him?"

"You mean besides just letting him drown?"

"Yes, besides that."

"Why, Nat? He's done so many wrongs in this situation I think letting him drown will give him time to think."

"If you did, then I'd be in trouble?"

"You?"

Natalie shrugged. "I already told him you'd help. You don't want me to take my word back, do you?"

Sixteen

What was he doing here? If anyone had told Jackson
two days ago he would be trying to help his family
member who obviously was trying to backstab him, he
would have laughed at them.

Natalie and he had gotten on the redeye to get home.
He had left her at her place and patted Obi on the head.
He nodded at Gina and said he'd be by later to pick up
Obi. Gina waved him off. Before he left, Natalie reached
out and cradled his chin.

"Remember Jackson, he's family."

Yes, that was exactly what Jackson was remembering
as he stood outside of the gym on the tenth floor in the
building. It totally amazed Jackson how Chris could be
coming to the gym to keep in shape after he'd put the
responsibility on Nat. The longer he waited, the angrier
he got.

As the people came out of the gym, some of them
stopped and gave him a second look. Jackson could tell
some people recognized him and gave him a nod, but
they didn't stop to talk to him. It made him think

Natalie may have a point. Maybe he needed to work on personnel interactions.

Outside of the gym, there was a small stand that advertised the coming of a wellness coach who would teach Tai Kwan do, tai chi, and yoga. Jackson looked at the listing and shook his head. It never amazed him how people could study all types of martial arts as relaxation. He had studied different defense techniques, and he had used most of them for their intended purpose, self-defense.

Jackson waited, trying to piece together what he had discovered. The reports on the finances, the projects that were suffering, and the clients that were affected. It was all starting to come together, and the realization of where it was pointing wasn't putting Jackson in a better mood.

"Jackson? I almost didn't recognize you in workout clothes."

Just the sound of his voice made him tired. He thought of all of the other really important things that needed to be done for the company. Then he pictured Natalie's face, and how concerned she was for Chris and how sure she was he could fix it, and met Chris as he walked out of the gym.

"Chris, we need to talk."

"About?"

"Let's go somewhere to discuss business. They keep a room inside for me."

Jackson walked Chris back into the gym. The front desk woman smiled and nodded at him as he walked by.

"I didn't know you came here, Jackson."

"I think there's a lot you don't know about me."

Jackson walked through the halls and went into a

room that had padded floors. He turned to look at Chris, who looked around the room, confused.

"What gives Jackson?"

"Natalie and I talked."

Chris walked slowly, and his eyes flitted towards the doorway.

"What did you talk about?"

Jackson tilted his head to one side as he looked at Chris.

"We talked about you," Jackson said quietly.

"She told you?"

"She told me that you were getting hustled."

"That's not true! I made a deal based on what I thought was going to happen, and it didn't pan out."

"And on your say-so alone, Marvin went ahead and gave you business that he valued for you?"

"He trusted me to make good on my promise when I got to be the head of the domestic division."

"If he trusts you for it and he knows that you'll pay for it, then what's the problem? Why does he need the money back now?"

Chris looked from side to side. "He put himself out for me, and now he needs to cover it. I need to give him back his money."

"It's amazing how honorable you are when it comes to dealing with Marvin, but you're willing to toss that aside to go to Natalie."

Chris ran his hands through his hair in frustration.

"I don't think you understand Jackson. I mean, she had some options and if she would have done those I'm sure—"

"Hold up. So you needed to preserve face in front of Marvin, but you wanted Natalie to go to Gran and lie for you?"

"It sounds bad, and I would have gone myself if I thought she would listen to me. Natalie was here a lot more than you were a year ago. She always dealt with Gran, and even when you two broke up, Gran kept an eye on Natalie."

"Does that mean you can use her because you lack the backbone to do your own work?" Jackson snarled.

Chris held up his hands. "Natalie can talk to anyone. It's a gift."

Jackson slowly advanced on Chris. "Tell me, Chris, how do you know how good she is at this type of negotiation? How many times have you asked her to interfere for you?"

"This was the first time I asked her to go to Gran for me," Chris stammered. "Marvin was calling me, and he kept threatening me that he would go and tell everyone that my contracts were no good."

"I bet he did, but instead of taking care of your problem, what wound up happening was you decided to pass it off to Natalie."

"Well—" Chris started to answer, but then his eyes locked with Jackson and he stopped.

"You see, you've created a problem for the both of us. At first, I thought I'd bring you in here and show you some moves that would sting a bit. Then I realized that Natalie would be unhappy with that. So what do you think, should I let the rumor out that you've been making false promises and then come in and save you?"

"Jackson, if you do that, they'll leave me and not trust me no matter what. You can't do that to me!" Chris started breathing fast and then looking around as if something or someone would come. "You think you can just come back, and it's all the way you left it?

Things move on and keep growing. You're old, and you should step aside for the new."

"You know what the sad thing is. This issue or problem that you got yourself into would have been the best thing to bring to Gran."

"What? She would have roasted me alive!"

"She would have laughed at you but then remembered we were all ambitious once and helped you."

"Or maybe I just need to find out if I can get Natalie to like me instead of you."

Before the words were completely out of his mouth, Jackson had thrown a right hook. Just as he threw the punch, the door opened.

It was a girl Jackson had never seen, but she covered her mouth and looked at Chris on the floor. "Oh my!" she exclaimed.

Jackson looked at her and smiled. "Hi, this is fine. It's a new communication plan."

When it didn't look like she was buying it, he reached down and pulled Chris up. All the while, keeping smiles on their faces. "Hey, make the young lady feel better and tell her this is part of the plan."

Chris got up and checked his jaw before saying through a grimace. "It's a new thing. He's done, so don't worry, I'm fine, thanks."

The woman gave them a second look, but as she saw the both of them smiling, she shook her head and turned. As she was leaving, they could hear her muttering "men."

The door closed, and Jackson turned to Chris. "Let's go get a drink."

"Personnel? That was the best thing you could come up with?" Chris said as they took a seat in the café in the building.

Jackson took a sip of his cola and then looked at Chris. "It was the first thing that came to mind because I've been told that I should work on it. Was it really that bad to call Natalie?"

"It was really that bad. I tried everything I knew. I wanted to renegotiate. I thought about getting a loan, but I couldn't get that kind of loan without someone knowing and signing off. What makes it worse is Marvin says he needs the money, but he'll take my shares in Connected to hold until I get the money, but I'm not comfortable with it. It looks like I may not have an option."

Jackson took a deep swallow of his cola and then looked at Chris sideways.

"What is it man? What are you thinking?" Chris asked, desperately.

"Hmm. I'm wondering if I was ever this naïve in business. I mean, we all start out knowing nothing, but I just can't remember that I was ever this bad."

Chris let his head fall onto the table, and he groaned out loud.

"Pull yourself together Chris. I'm going to help you out."

Chris picked up his head. "You're going to give me the money?"

"No, but I'm going to show you how to handle snakes even when they look nice and innocent. Data beats everything. We're going to review the data, and then we can move forward."

"Data?"

"Yes, we're going to look at data in all of its forms so you can go from the hunted, to the hunter."

Seventeen

Natalie's phone pinged with a text from Jackson, *Sorry, can't do lunch.*

You okay? she sent back.

Personnel issues.

Be friendly, don't threaten, she warned.

Buying drinks offering advice.

Good job! I knew you could do this!

Personnel issues are top of my list.

Thanks for being open.

Natalie had never been invited to Howard's center. She knew that he was doing new work with kids but hadn't ever seen it. When she received the invite that afternoon, she decided she'd go. When she walked into the building, she was immediately greeted by a woman who stood in the spacious lobby with an iPad under her arm. The woman waited patiently for Natalie to come further into the lobby.

Natalie walked slowly toward the young woman, distracted by the surroundings. On the walls, there were holographic pictures of children smiling. The frames themselves appeared to change color, as well. The frames were delicately made and everything from the walls, to the pictures to even the tiles she walked on with every other one having a child's face on it. If nothing else, Natalie could tell Howard was dedicated to helping children.

She was finally face to face with the greeter.

"Can I help you?"

"I'm here to see Howard Banner," Natalie said.

The greeter gave Natalie a long look. Natalie looked back at the young woman who looked to be in her mid-twenties with a fresh face that made her look like she had just come out of high school.

"I'm sorry, but Mr. Banner doesn't see people here."

Natalie smiled and reached for her phone. She was looking up Howard's number when she heard Beth's voice.

"I'm so glad you came. I mean, you're technically late, but you came," Beth said as she approached. "I wasn't sure if you'd be able to come."

Natalie looked at her email quickly and then back at Beth. "I thought Howard was going to meet me?"

"No, it was me. I sent the message. You wouldn't believe how many people don't feel comfortable when I invite them, but when Howard does, it's like Christmas." Beth said as her mouth tightened with tension and disbelief.

Beth looked at the greeter, and the greeter took a step back. Beth waved Natalie on to follow her and spoke as she walked down the hall.

"Those greeters are just overpaid eye candy. I don't know why Howard thinks we need them. Anyway, the reason I needed you here is I'm worried about Lori."

"I saw Lori in the office. I think she's feeling a little tense with Jackson here, but she seemed okay."

"Well, that just shows how you don't know Lori," Beth quipped. "There is something not right with her. Do you know she was translating and slipped into another language? She never loses her concentration like that. I've asked her, and she won't say there is anything wrong, but I know there is. The fact that she and Chris have been talking was the final straw that I needed. The last time those two had their heads together, Chris owed money."

Natalie sighed now, understanding how it was all making sense. Rob had said he'd seen Lori talking to the business contact, and Chris had already told her about the money problem he was having. Still, she wasn't sure that Lori wasn't having any problems, so she kept her council.

"You think that Lori would give money to Chris and not tell you?"

"I hope not, but they're siblings, and they would stand with each other to try to save each other from the old woman."

Natalie smiled. "It seems like a lot of things go on in the name of saving oneself from Gran."

They had finally made it to her office, where she had a small couch, and they both took a seat.

Beth gave her a long look. "I hope you're not still upset with Lori for not telling you what was in the box?"

"No, Beth, I'm fine. It really hasn't been on my mind."

"Well, that's good. You know she did what she had to do for the sake of being loyal to family and all that."

"I guess that makes it all better right? Banners may fight in all sorts of ways, but at the end of the day, they stick together no matter what or who."

Beth sat back on the couch and sighed. "I have to agree with Lori. You were fortunate that day didn't work out for you. Jackson is a beast of a man and even worse now that he's decided to come back and be the CEO. We're all suffering, and we suffered horribly for months after you left. Yes, yes, you were the lucky one."

"I can see how you would think that was the most important part of this whole event," Natalie agreed wryly.

"Jackson is always full of secrets. We never knew what he was going to do, and if he ever told us anything, we had to keep it to ourselves. Jackson is the master of controlling everything, and it puts us all in a bind to have to follow him."

"That is a very Banner view of things." Natalie cleared her throat and stared at Beth. "Jackson and secrets don't do well, and it doesn't do well when people try to interfere in his business. All that being said, if Lori had any problems, especially with money, wouldn't she tell someone. Are you sure it's a money problem?"

"Well, what I can tell you is that she's taken a loan out against one of her properties."

"How can you know that for sure?"

Beth smiled and looked at Natalie. "You never stop being a mother. I've got some friends who watch over their investments. I watch over Lori's investments. Chris's are international. International banks aren't very understanding of motherly love."

"So just for argument's sake, let's assume that you are right. What do you expect me to do?"

"I want you to find out what's wrong with Lori and make sure she's okay. I have done all I can do. Now, you need to do the other part."

Natalie stared at her and had to close her mouth at the gall. "Why would you think I have to do something?"

"Well, if not you, then Jackson."

"Have you told Jackson?"

Beth looked flustered. "No, that's why I called you. Whatever the problem is, it will probably need more money than what she has. You can talk to Jackson, and I'm sure Jackson or the old woman will give you the money. No one doubts your loyalty to the old woman. The both of you are close. She'd probably be happier if you were family, but we all have to live with disappointments."

Natalie fell back on the sofa. "I'm so lost as to why you can't go to Sherry?"

Beth harrumphed. "You're lost because you have nothing to lose. Every time Lori or Chris have done something, she's been furious. She watches accounts and then lets everyone know that this last event is the reason that they are not going to ever run the company. She doesn't tolerate mistakes."

Natalie sighed. "I know she can be…difficult."

Beth clenched her jaw and blinked back what looked to be tears. "When it comes to my family, we are not looked on kindly. She wanted Howard to go into business, but it wasn't his calling. She blames us for letting Lori and Chris get into financial trouble. You should have heard her say if we had spent more time on business and less time on therapy, maybe we'd have true Banners."

"That sounds like her," Natalie said with a sad smile.

"There is nothing amusing here, Natalie. If the old woman finds out that my kids are costing her money, she might disown all of us."

"I do know that she can be strict and stern, but you are all still family. She won't disown you."

"Really? We don't have any real value to her anyway. Jackson is back. He's a real Banner. He's someone she can talk to, and they have so much in common."

"I can understand your concern, but Jackson and her are only close because there is a problem in the company. She still wants to keep the rest of the family. She's just focusing on one thing at a time."

Beth shook her head. "She'd do whatever was best for the company. Getting rid of some people would be a reasonable sacrifice to maintain all that she has. She was married once. All of the relatives from her husband's side tried to get money, and she disowned them."

Natalie thought about it. "I hadn't really thought about other relatives."

"Yes, well, you can't think about people who aren't around."

"I suppose that fight was long and bitter."

"It wasn't either. Sherry got the case pushed back and then offered a settlement during the wait. I learned something that day. No one is safe, and the most important thing to her is the company."

"I'm sorry, Beth. Now I have to ask, after realizing that the company would always be the most important thing and that Howard wasn't very company orientated, you still married him?"

"I know what they say about me. That I'm pushy and that I'm bossy. They wonder why Howard married me. When I met Howard, he was trying to learn the business. What he wound up doing was counseling the staff. I loved him enough to stay. When I met Sherry Banner, she was ready to beat Howard into a mold."

"So, you married Howard to help him?"

"No, I married him because I love him just the way he is. I didn't want the world to lose that, and I couldn't imagine my life without him. The Howard I know is a gift not just to me but to a lot of kids as well," Beth said with a sniff and then blinked away the moisture that was building in her eyes.

"Looking around, I can definitely see Howard has found his passion," Natalie sympathized.

"Howard dreams of getting businesses to support children in therapy. Working families face the largest challenges when it comes to children. It's a hard place to stand, between Sherry and Howard. She wants profits, and he wants to save the kids. I was hoping she'd be able to look at one of the kids, and they'd have an aptitude for business. While I think they do, every mistake they made was a strike against them because they'd always be compared to Jackson."

"I'm sorry, Beth. You have to know your kids are great in business, just learning the ropes like everyone."

"So you say but what she says is, When Jackson opened his own side company, and it was a success, and he sold it, he solidified his spot as a money maker. When he left last year, I thought maybe it was an opportunity. Maybe Jackson was gone for good, and he'd come back to relinquish his role and then Chris would have a chance. As it has turned out, the boy genius was only taking a break."

Natalie let Beth finish, and when the silence had grown, she jumped in. "You're sure the issue is money with Lori?"

"I'm pretty sure. I can make some discreet calls to confirm."

"Would you please?"

Beth reached out and took Natalie's hand. "Thank you, Natalie. I knew if I could talk to you, you'd understand and help me. Please, I'm trusting you to keep this family business private."

"Of course."

"Do you want some dessert and coffee?"

Those were the words he tossed at her as she walked out of the building. Natalie nodded, thinking it would be a great time to tell him about Lori. When she sat in the car, she could tell his mood was not as carefree as she originally thought.

"How was personnel today?" she asked.

"I think it went fine. I spoke to Chris, and I believe we now understand each other."

"I think that's great," Natalie sat back and sifted through the day, trying to find the words to give Jackson. "I was worried that you wouldn't be able to get past his error and help him to move on."

"No, I'm taking your advice dealing with personnel, personally."

Natalie turned to her side and looked at Jackson. His profile was strong, and confidence just oozed off of him. It was no surprise to her that they all knew he had the answers.

She wanted to reach out and touch him. To trace the strong chords of his throat down to his broad shoulders and over the curves of the muscles in his arms. He moved his body so effortlessly, and when she saw him, she saw someone who was strong and capable. Someone, she could be safe with.

Shaking her head to clear it of Jackson, she said, "So, what's the plan?"

"Chris is going to get the plan together."

Natalie paused. "You're helping him though, right?"

Jackson nodded. "But you know Nat in these situations people have to have some latitude. They don't learn unless they can do some things on their own. Chris will work to get himself out of this, so he'll recognize it when he sees it again."

"If you help him take care of it, though, will he still see it again?"

"If he wants to stay in business, this will come again in many forms. He has to learn how not to panic. Not to be pushed and how to take his own hits if that's the case."

"Are you going to show him at least an outline?"

"I gave him all I was given, and he'll have to work it out or ask me."

"Seems easier to help him solve it."

"It actually is easier for me, but I want him to do this, and it will give me a chance to understand how he thinks."

"Well, he must be relieved you know what you're doing, and he has someone to go to."

"I gave him work, but I didn't tell him that I had it all worked out. This is business, he needs to make his own way," Jackson said tightly.

Natalie stopped. "You know this is a worry to him. Why not tell him—"

"Tell him what, Nat? Not to worry, that I've cleaned up his mess? No. I gave him steps, and he needs to do them, and then he'll know what to do and how to do it. He'll be a better man for it."

Natalie wasn't sure she agreed with the technique, but she had to remember Jackson knew how to handle one of his own.

"Are you still investigating?"

"I am. Some things just don't match up."

"You still think the company problems are done from the inside. You're in a minority when it comes to liking Gran. She's an acquired taste, and it appears that some people haven't been able to get past her first impression."

Natalie thought on all of the family members she had visited, and it appeared that they could have all been angry enough to do something, but embezzlement just seemed extreme. She was going to bring up Lori, but then the car stopped, and they were in front of Jackson's place.

"We're here, let's hit the sweets," Jackson said with a devilish grin.

Eighteen

Jackson had been waiting all day to see Natalie. In fact lately, he caught himself looking round to catch a glimpse of her in the office. When they had missed lunch, he immediately thought of another plan in order to see her and cashing in on their coffee date.

Jackson wondered what Natalie saw? He lived in a one-bedroom coop in a 25 story building with a doorman. He had lived in a home before, but it didn't seem practical for all of the traveling he did.

The layout was a large room that opened into his living room, and then behind it was a wall that separated the kitchen and the dining table. There was a hallway on the far right that led to the back and his bedroom.

He had already bought the desserts and set up the dining room table. He tried to get an assortment, not knowing what she liked. When they had been together before, they had lots of dinners and cocktails, but the little things that couples did like coffee and pastry shops had been missing.

Jackson took her coat and laid it on the sofa. Then he guided her to the kitchen where he saw a smile light up her face and knew he had made the right decision.

She turned to him with a smile on her face. "Wow, you wanted to make sure I had a good time, I see. The selection is great!"

"If we are putting our cards on the table. I wasn't sure what your favorite was, so I got a spread."

"Well, pat yourself on the back. Three of my favs are here." She sat down and looked longingly at the pastries.

"Go ahead. It's just us. I won't tell a soul."

"Hmm. Maybe that will work," she muttered to herself. Natalie lifted her head and looked at Jackson.

"I don't think I can do this," she said regretfully.

"Do what? Eat all you want? Go ahead. I like a woman who eats."

She gave him a stern look and then shook her head. "No, work on this relationship thing." She looked around the kitchen before turning back to him. "I think it's a problem us trying to work on us and you trying to fix the problems at Connected."

Jackson stopped. He never considered she'd say no. Jackson had plans upon plans on how to address things, but Natalie just not wanting to participate wasn't one of them.

"Nothing new has happened, so why now?"

She was chewing her bottom lip and clasping her hands. "I don't want to go through the public mud again. Banners have a way of going through others and leaving bodies in their wake."

Jackson had done everything he could to reassure her, but he knew this was a risk that only time could fix, and time wasn't on his side. "What is it, are doubting my intentions towards you or if I have any feelings for you?"

She pushed away from the table and stood up. "I don't see the point in answering this."

He stood, and they were face to face. "I think there is a point in answering it. I think I'm due an answer."

He saw her chest rise and fall from her deep breaths. Her eyes were narrowing, and her lips were closed as if she were fighting herself to respond to the question.

"I'm doubting both," she said in a low voice. "There it is. It's both. I'm scared that this is just another moment for you to make sure you can get the girl who walked away. Maybe it's about your ego, maybe…maybe I don't know what it's about. Whatever it is, I don't want to do it in public for the King's pleasure!"

"The King, huh? I didn't think you'd listen to that kind of gossip."

She stepped away from him and sat back down. "They all do whatever it is that you want."

"Because I'm right about business doesn't make me a king."

"I can't be one of your public projects."

"You're not a project."

"Then what is going on here?"

Jackson reached out and caressed her cheek. "I know this is scary. It's scary for us both. I'll do whatever I can to make sure this isn't a public experience, but don't give up on me because of hearsay."

She took a breath and nodded. Then she offered him a pastry from the box. She took a bite and smiled.

Jackson wondered if she knew how amazing she was to him. Natalie was upfront and honest about her feelings. She had the courage to face him with her insecurities. He knew she was the woman who would always be there for the person she decided to support and love.

He took a bite out of the vanilla pastry and then laid it on the paper plate that was in front of him. "So, what do you think we can do about this issue of me publicly courting you?"

Natalie coughed and cleared her throat. When she had recovered, she looked at him and laughed. "I think you need to warn me before you say things like that. I almost choked on my donut."

"What was the joke?"

"Publicly courting?"

"Yes, I'm letting my feelings show and getting to know you, and you decide if it works for you or not, also known as public courting."

She finished her pastry and licked her fingertips. "Okay, you're coming up with all of these odd definitions to get me to leave some pastries. You make it sound like it's all about what I want."

"Because it is."

She looked at him with an exaggerated brow.

Jackson gave her a slow smile. "If this had been about my pacing, we might have done things a bit differently."

"Really?"

"Really."

"Okay, your majesty, what would have been different?"

He stood up and walked towards her and held out his hand. "Trust me."

She looked at his hand and then his face. Then she slowly put a trembling hand in his. He pulled her into his arms and let the smell of vanilla surround him.

"You always smell like vanilla."

"It's my soap," she said nervously.

"I think it's you. Sometimes when I'm traveling, and

I smell it, I think I need to wrap up business and get back."

Jackson moved his hands along her shoulder blades and felt her stiffen in his embrace.

"Nothing is happening here without you, and everything stops when you say so. I might be the King at the company, but you should know you're my Queen, and you rule all the time."

She looked him in the eye and gave him a wan smile.

"Oh yeah you're really putting it on thick. This doesn't mean that you're getting an extra pastry, though."

He felt her body relax, and he smiled back. Jackson was moved by her ability to adjust as she went. She managed to touch him in new ways that he didn't think he could be touched.

"I'd like to kiss you," he said. "You can say no, or you can knee me and leave," he grinned. "I'm hoping you'll go with the no option as the first choice."

"I won't do either. You can kiss me, Jackson."

He had to admit he was hoping that this was going to be a more spontaneous moment, but he wasn't one to let an opportunity go by. Jackson felt himself tremble and a new nervousness he hadn't felt since he'd opened his first company or kissed his first girl.

He brushed her mouth once, and there was nothing but vanilla cream. The second time he brushed her lips, he felt her hands slide up his chest, and wrap around his neck. She settled into his arms, and he kissed her. It didn't take more than she was willing to give. When he lifted his head, they stayed that way for several seconds, looking at one another. She parted her lips, and just when he thought she would lean in towards him, she surprised him.

"So, I guess you want the jelly donut now?"

They both laughed, and he let her go. They took their seats, and he split the jelly donut between them.

"So about us Jackson."

He held up his donut as he spoke, and Natalie smiled at him. "I'm courting you now. As long as we are both clear. Those are my intentions."

"We're so different," she warned.

"It's like a balance sheet. You need credits and debits. We're fine."

"I don't want this to interfere with work," Natalie explained.

"I think we're fine. No one is aware that I multi-task, trying to get you to trust me and take a chance on us."

Natalie smiled and blued. "I don't mean that. I mean, I don't want to explain our private lives to everyone I meet at Connected. I also mean it with Gina. I work with Gina, you know."

"So, you want to sneak around?"

"No, I'm saying we could be a little less public and more discreet? Jackson don't look at me that way!"

"We're adults!"

He watched her lift her chin and set her jaw and knew that statement wasn't the best way to go, but it was too late to pull it back.

"If we can't figure this out—"

Jackson threw up his hands. "Fine, we'll do this your way. I'll be—what did you say?—discreet, for now."

Natalie gave him a hesitant glance. "For now?"

"Remember what I said. You're the Queen, and you always rule."

Nineteen

"I know something you would like to know," Catherine said from the doorway of Natalie's office.

"Since you are supposedly my assistant, I hope that situation is only temporary," replied Natalie.

"Sherry has called Jackson in for an update."

Natalie jumped up from her desk and gave Catherine a hug.

"I'm going to remember you when it's time for the bonuses," Natalie threw over her shoulder.

"I'm counting on it!"

Natalie went into the hallway, looked both ways, and then went in next door. "Jackson?"

"Come in, Natalie," Jackson replied.

Jackson was still at his desk when he looked up, and a slow smile spread across his face. Just when Natalie was about to speak, Catherine bustled in.

"Oh, Mr. Banner, your Gran wants to see you in her office."

With that announcement, Catherine left, and Jackson smiled at Natalie.

"So, it looks like you're going to Gran."

Jackson sighed. "It's true. She wants to be kept up to date. I am the CEO because she and the family backs me. I think the bid to have me removed is taking a back seat to me finding the person causing problems."

Natalie went to his door and closed it and then took the seat in front of his desk. "Jackson, have you told her you think it's a family member?"

"No, just that I'm doing an investigation. Until I know exactly who it is, I won't give her any false targets. But I think she should know my thoughts."

"Allow for the possibility that you could be wrong."

Jackson scoffed. "Okay."

Natalie glared. "Pretend it's possible. Until we have all the facts, I can't believe there is anyone in your family who would deliberately do anything to the company to put it in danger. I think if you hint at such a thing, it will put Gran in a fitful frame of mind that could make her go on a witch hunt that no one wants."

"Okay, Ms. Personnel, I'm interested in your solution."

"I think we need to think out of the box," Natalie said, waving her hands in the air. "Perhaps what we want to do is to give the high-level picture without indulging in any specifics. Of course, make it known that you are handling the situation."

"I don't know Nat, this sounds suspiciously like not telling the truth," Jackson said with a grin on his face. "Is this how we forge better relations with personnel?"

"Jackson! Don't play. I'm not telling you to make anything up. You are working on finding the truth. You don't have all the facts. You believe you have some good leads, but you said it yourself you don't know. Also, while we are on the subject of what you should discuss, I want to say that I don't think it should be necessary to talk about Chris' problem. They already have a strained relationship, and since he's taking care of it, I don't think it bears mentioning."

Jackson sat back in his chair and gave Natalie a long look. "This doesn't seem to be the kind of advice I'd expect from you. So I'm supposed to tell her there is a problem but not who I suspect?"

"Yes, that about sums it up."

"And on top of that, I'm not supposed to mention the issue with Chris either, is that correct?"

"Yes, that too."

Jackson folded his hands over his chest and leaned back in his chair. "What else would you like me to not talk about?"

Natalie looked at him with crossed arms and then nodded.

Jackson opened his hands and nodded. "You're the Queen."

She smiled at him. "I think I'm liking that."

"Well, with great powers come great responsibility."

"What?" She asked, looking at him as if he had lost his mind.

"I'm willing to do what you're asking, but since we have to be discreet, I wanted to know if you could schedule some time for a coffee date."

Natalie was outraged. "I can't believe you'd ask such a thing."

Jackson smiled and looked unrepentant.

"I wish it was true that I was as honorable as you, but I'm just a lowly man trying to court a woman to give me a second glance. I'd like a small thing. A little bit of her time. I'd provide some food and show her I can be what she's dreaming of."

Natalie blushed. "You want me to agree to a date?"

"Yes, just a little bit of your time."

Natalie looked at the ceiling and rolled her eyes. "This is ridiculous, but fine I agree. We can go on a date."

"You act like I don't date," Jackson said with a laugh.

"Let's just say I don't imagine you dating."

"Oh, and what do you think happens?"

"I imagine you walk in, and women throw themselves at you."

Jackson laughed. "I like listening to other people's ideas of what they think happens in my life. Their versions are so much better than the truth."

Jackson got up and started to the door. He stopped by Natalie and leaned in close to her.

"Just so we're clear. My redacted report and our date."

"I'm not guaranteeing anything. I'm just saying yes to dinner."

"The rest, as you say, is up to me. That I've got." Then he leaned in just an inch more and kissed her on the cheek. With that, he walked out of his office. When the door had closed behind him, she sat down and thought about what she had done. Jackson and his courting was becoming unpredictable, erratic, and weirdly exciting. She thought if she put an obstacle or two in front of him, he would stop and find something or someone else, but he had pleasantly surprised her at every turn.

This was not the Jackson she knew. This was a Jackson that she didn't know. He confused her with his antics, but he intrigued her with his persistence. She thought about waiting in his office but who knew how long that meeting would take? Just as she was going towards the door, Chris walked in.

"Do I have the right office?" Chris asked.

Natalie saw a happy Chris, and she greeted him with a smile.

"You are in the right office. You just missed him, and I was just leaving."

"I can hang out with you for a bit if you have time."

"Sure, Chris, take a seat. I'm sure Jackson won't mind us using his office. So tell me, what brings you here?"

"I wanted to let him know that it's all going well with the investor." Chris sat in the chair and leaned back. Natalie could see the confidence in him and knew asking Jackson had been the right thing. "Jackson was right. I needed to get my information on everything, and I would know how he was just trying to herd me into a bad decision."

"So you're not worried that he'll ruin your reputation, or you'll have to pay money?"

"No, if anything, he would end up in jail for what he was trying to do."

"I'm so relieved. You can't possibly know how worried I was about you."

Chris laughed. "We're both relieved. I'm glad I have a plan and got this moving. I'd hate for Jackson to have to go through with any of the things he threatened to end my career with."

Natalie stopped and inched closer to Chris. "I'm sorry, I must have misheard you."

Chris was laughing and didn't notice how still Natalie was or how close she was moving to him.

"Yeah, Jackson was really angry. He was going to let my reputation get slaughtered and then save me. It would have been too late by then, but instead, he gave me this option."

"I'm so glad he gave you this option as well. Thank you so much, Chris. I think Jackson will be in his meeting for a bit, but I'll let him know you were here."

Chris left the office smiling, and Natalie walked into her office and decided she'd breathe and wait. He couldn't stay with Gran all day.

Twenty

"I'd like to speak to you if you have a moment, Jackson."

He knew who it was even before she spoke. However, today his Queen had a little bit of an edge to her voice.

"Of course."

"I'd like you to look at me if you please," Natalie said as she dropped into the seat in front of him.

"You don't look happy, and I assure you I followed your advice to the letter."

"Did you? I wonder, did you follow my advice when it came to Chris? Did you have a nice conversation with him and help him with his trouble."

Jackson knew where this was going. It occurred to him he'd never really had the experience of being on the receiving end of a dressing down. He supposed if he told her how attractive she looked as she was preparing to go to war, that she wouldn't take that well at all. Instead, he sat back and watched her get ready to take the King down. He'd try to get a word in before she started though.

"First, I didn't threaten him. There wasn't one thing I said to him that I wasn't prepared to let happen to him."

"Jackson, I sent you to help him!"

Natalie moved so she could pace in front of his desk.

"I did help him. Just ask him."

"After you made threats against his livelihood?" she asked.

"Okay, there were some items we had to address."

"Jackson, threatening people isn't the way you do things."

"And taking advantage of those around you isn't either. He needs to know how to stand on his own two feet. That lesson had to be taught first, and then I had to show him how to get out of his predicament."

Natalie stopped pacing. "Why didn't you tell me that you had to threaten him?"

"You sent me to fix Chris. I did that. You didn't say come back and report what happened," he said as evenly as he could.

She shook her head and looked at him through weary eyes. "Yes, I wanted the problem fixed, but I don't want him to have worse habits from the fix. What am I going to do with you, Jackson?"

"Well, the first thing I suggest is an old-fashioned thank you. The second thing I think is that you could say you're ready for our date."

Jackson watched her struggle with the pros and cons, but in the end, she took a breath and gave the fair answer.

"I guess you're right. I don't like the way you did it, but you did do what I asked."

"There were no conditions on the task. You just wanted it done. So if we are both agreed on item one, then we must be ready for item two?"

"Item two? It's the middle of the day practically. We can't just leave work."

Jackson walked to Natalie and offered his hand. She put her hand in his and then looked at him waiting. He was thrilled she had put her hand in his without waiting. He was making progress. She'd put her hand in his first and ask questions later.

"As it happens. I have it on good authority that even Queens are allowed lunch," he said with a smile.

"It looks like we're outside," she said.

"It's supposed to. It's a personal grotto," Jackson said as he poured them fruit drinks.

Natalie looked at the glass and then back at him. "We're drinking?"

"Call me arrogant, I didn't think I needed the liquor. This is about us and romance, not about too much wine going to our heads and either one of us having an excuse as to why it did or didn't go right."

Jackson hadn't given her much time. She had just put on her out-to-lunch message on her outlook and picked up her id when she saw him standing at her office door. She was excited and nervous at the same time.

Now it seemed like it was all coming together. He was almost done with the investigation, and he had agreed to her terms about being discreet. Now that all those items were out of the way, Natalie had nothing to stand in her way of thinking about them.

Her anticipation was going up because each time Jackson had found a way to tease the woman out and give him a little more trust. As they had walked out of the building, the memory of their kiss still stirred her and made her wonder what else was there.

They sat in the restaurant grotto, and the waiter had already brought them a platter of cold appetizers and cheeses. The place was comfortable. She had to say that. It was a soft booth that was curved to force a couple to sit closely. The booth itself extended to a half-moon so that no one could see inside unless they came in. In the restaurant, no two booths faced each other directly, making it seem like they had even more privacy.

She took the glass and took a sip. The fruit juice was sweet and welcoming. It somehow calmed the butterflies in her stomach. She looked around and then back at him.

"I know I agreed to a date, but this seems a bit over the top. I mean it must be a—"

His eyebrow rose. "Try to turn off the project manager brain for a moment. We're not on a business deal, and we won't have to figure out who will pay for this or where it will be expensed."

"Okay," she said and looked at him over the glass.

He laughed and moved closer to her.

"In case you didn't know, one of the things that I really like about you is that you have a strong work ethic. I think you hide in it like I hide in making companies and money. It takes a special kind of person to understand that kind of behavior."

She heard him and knew he was thinking about his parents. She reached out and touched his arm that was between them. He was strong and warm. She thought she was going to feel awkward on this date. Instead, she was able to relax into him.

"It's true, being driven and passionate about what you do isn't always understood. It can be tough on everyone."

Jackson raised his glass. "Not to me. I toast dedication and passion."

She looked at him. "The restaurant is nice."

Jackson laughed. "You think it's nice. It's supposed to put you in the mood and help my cause."

"You don't need help, Jackson."

He leaned in closer and stopped right before his lips touched hers. "May I?"

She knew he would want to kiss her again. If she were honest, she'd say that she was waiting for him to do it again. Then she nodded and a bloom of feeling engulfed her.

He lowered his head and kissed her. It went from playing with words to the feel of his mouth on hers. She was lost in the shadow of his kiss. The kiss was just as good as the last. She could hear her heartbeat, and it seemed to slow to synchronize with his. When she felt his arms go around her, she melted into his embrace and indulged in the kiss she wished would never end.

His lips were light and moved across hers, luring her with the taste of what could be. Then she shifted to be closer to him and trailed her hands up until they were on his shoulders. His arms tightened and then she heard it.

"Oh!"

She stiffened in his embrace for a moment, and the kiss ended but they were still head to head.

"I think I'm going to kill the waiter," Jackson whispered.

"I think I'm going to tip him big time. We are in a restaurant."

They both turned to see a red-faced young man bringing a carafe of drinks.

"I-I-I am so sorry. I'll go—" the waiter stammered.

The moment was broken but not forgotten. The lunch went on with them talking about the appetizers and the grotto. The occasional looks Jackson gave her made her smile like she was in high school. The way he touched her as he fixed her plate or the subtle brushes of his hand as he refilled her juice were an extension of the kiss and seemed to bank the feeling she had for him. When the lunch was done, he brought her back to the office.

"Thank you, my Queen."

"Jackson?"

"You don't need to respond. I just wanted to say thank you."

Twenty-one

An alert on Natalie's phone notified her of a new text from Jackson. *I hear you've been summoned.*

Yes, I'm at the door.

Do you need backup?

It's Gran.

Ah, I've heard the innocent can go near and she doesn't bite.

Natalie smile at that, *Really? You're so dramatic.*

No I'm looking out for you. It's hard to keep a treasure.

What do you want smooth-talker?

I was thinking about visiting Obi tonight?

I should charge you boarding fees.

His reply was quick, *I'll pay if I get visitation.*

Whatever.

I'll see you later my Queen.

The good news was Gran was very lively today. The bad news was she was ready to rip Jackson apart. Natalie smiled and thought on Jackson's words about dedication and passion. She had been invited for tea at Gran's house. Again they were in the sitting room where Jackson's welcome party had been. As usual, Gran was dressed to the nine's. She had on a peach, pastel blouse with full sleeves and a sash at her neck. She topped it off with a black skirt with peach peonies on it.

"So what is Jackson doing? He had to give me a report and he said absolutely nothing for twenty minutes. He droned on about an investigation but couldn't give me any details."

Natalie picked up her cup and drank some tea. Well, he had for once done exactly what she had said and this was the result. Maybe she would defer to him more to avoid these kinds of situations.

"He's working with personnel very closely and I think it's building his trust relationships."

Gran put her tea down and looked at Natalie. "Do you think I care what he's doing with personnel? I want results. Does he think he can just throw anything my way and I'll accept it. Maybe I'm the feeble one to endure him at all."

"I'm sure that Jackson is close to fixing things and I think we should give him a little more time."

"Time? Does it look like I have a lot of time," Gran said as she begrudgingly took a sip of tea. After she put her cup down, Gran smoothed her skirt, straightened her back and gave Natalie a firm look. "Now, Natalie I need to talk with you about a matter and I want your unfettered input."

"Yes?" The way this was being asked put Natalie on edge but she tried not to get too nervous.

"You know I've always helped you because I felt as though you are an amazing talent and it was a personal and professional loss for Connected to lose you. When I needed to bring Jackson back I asked your company to get you here. You weren't very receptive asking Jackson back, for obvious reasons, but do you still feel that I should have left him alone?"

Natalie put her tea down and tried to hide the shock she felt at the question. If Gran was asking this question then the money and the problems must be larger than what she imagined.

"You're right. I wasn't sure I wanted to face Jackson again for anything and I've been very fortunate for all of the good words that you've put in for me. When it comes to Jackson well, he is still a Banner through and through. He's eccentric but he can fix what is wrong with Connected."

"You mean if he wants to save it at all," Gran said. "It wasn't until the party that I realized how much anger the family had against him. Maybe he knew all along and he has another plan."

"I'm sorry?"

Gran reached out and patted Natalie's hand.

"You know it's hard to see in someone else something you wouldn't do. However, I have to say that I've wondered, and it came to me again that maybe he was coming back to get back at us for wanting to remove him as CEO. He's young and his pride might have been offended. He wouldn't be the first to go back home to tear it down and build something better."

"Gran, he knows you supported him as the CEO. I don't think any of the others are pushing this idea of removing him either. I want you to know if I saw anything in his behavior that said he was going to hurt the company, I'd tell you."

"Then where are my results?"

Natalie had to hide her smile. She wondered if Gran knew how alike she was with Jackson.

"He'll deliver."

Gran sniffed. "I hope he gets it together Natalie. I understand he may not like the idea of having to answer to me. None of the others do. In fact, I guess I should be happy we are living in this day and age. Otherwise, they might ambush me to get the company."

"Gran!"

Gran waved her away. "I know they deal with me because of the money. Elizabeth is a viper waiting to strike."

"I think Elizabeth and you have a lot in common. You both want to protect your families. She does it the same way you do, she puts herself out there first as a target."

Gran sat back and looked at Natalie. "I'll have to think that one over. I don't know if I can credit that much love and compassion to her."

Natalie reached out and touched Gran's hand. "She loves Howard and what he does. She knows that Howard isn't in the family business but he still needs your support. She wants him to be able to be himself."

"And what? I would stop that?"

"You could disown him."

"What foolishness!"

Natalie sat back. "I don't think so. Just think about it from their point of view. Recently, there was a possibility that you all would ask Jackson to step down as CEO and he's making the company money."

"He was!"

Natalie held up her hands. "Gran, Jackson has some immediate value to you, what does Howard?"

Gran looked around the house and sighed. "You know everything you see around you is for my family. It's true I'm stern but it's to make sure there is something left for them later. I haven't understood why Howard wants to work with children. This company is for my children and his!"

"I hear you Gran, but you found your way to give to your children. Let Howard have his," Natalie said. "Parenting doesn't come with instructions. We all value something different. I think the best thing we can do is understand what the other values, and try to love each other."

"Values. You're right we all value something but I sacrificed a lot for this company. I had the love of my life with me and I had to work at this company," Gran said in a stern voice. "We dreamed that this company would be our legacy to the kids. We didn't want the money it made. I didn't care one way or the other. My husband did. He wanted there to be more than just us. When you talk about sacrifice and values. The opportunity for me to be me and live the life I wanted was sacrificed at the feet of my children. It's hard to see them throw that back at me and say 'no thank you.'"

"I know you were dedicated to the company but I thought you loved the business," Natalie whispered.

Gran looked at Natalie with tears glistening in her eyes.

"No child, I didn't love the business but I loved the man who wanted to leave this for others to remember him by. Day and night he taught me everything that I needed to know. I learned those things like they were pearls. I promised him I'd do this and when he passed, a part of me passed with him. I understand there are things that we all want to do but sometimes we need to do what the family needs. Jackson understands this and so should Howard and Elizabeth."

"Gran, Jackson loves working in the business. That's not fair to Howard."

Gran looked sadly at Natalie. "You're right it's not fair. So for all of our sakes, I hope your faith hasn't been misplaced. In the end, we don't do what's fair but what's right for the family."

Natalie sighed. "Jackson will fix this. I can tell you from experience he will fix it the way he wants to, but he will fix it."

"He's hiding stuff from me," Gran muttered.

"Remember, you wanted to save the business. If you wanted someone to direct, Jackson was not the person to call. In fact, he has a very negative reaction to being told what to do."

"So you're saying we have to go along for the ride and hope for the best?"

"No, I'm saying you have to go along for the ride and hold on. He'll get you there but we'll be going at his speed."

"Well look who's here," Gina said, with Obi in her arms. "It's the legendary King himself. We are so happy to invite you to our humble abode. We're having lasagna. Eat small portions, I want some for lunch."

The smell of cheese and sauce wafted in the air. Jackson smiled, used to Gina and her love for food. "How many trays did she make?"

"One for tonight and one for tomorrow, certainly you can see the shortage. What will we feed Obi and me during our midnight snack?" Gina smiled as she hugged Obi closer to herself.

"I think you'll survive," Jackson said as he walked in. He had a bottle of wine and Gina exchanged Obi for the wine bottle.

Obi stayed in his arms for a moment and then wiggled to get down. As soon as he was on the floor he went straight to the kitchen. "So much for her discipline," muttered Jackson.

As he walked to the kitchen he thought about Natalie and her call earlier. She had told him Gina was staying in and if he wanted to he could cancel. He could hear it in her voice that he would but he told her it wouldn't be a problem. Gina was a part of her life as well.

"Look at this he brought some sweet fruity juice in a wine bottle. Are pickings hard Jackson?" Gina teased.

Gina gave Natalie the bottle, she looked at it and then he smiled.

"The juice is from a grotto," he said. Natalie blushed and took the bottle to keep working on dinner.

"Ew! Is that some hidden meaning stuff between the two of you? I think I may have to eat in front of the television with Obi," Gina quipped.

Jackson looked at Natalie, dressed in jeans and a soft pink tank top. When he was next to her she looked at him and a light blush was still on her cheeks.

"Thanks for coming."

"You think I'd let something come between me and my Queen?" he whispered.

"Enough, take a seat. You're probably just buttering me up to get ready for you leaving Obi with me."

"I don't know if Obi will ever want to be with me again," Jackson said as he brought dishes to the table. "He knows a good thing when he's found it. Although I admit it's been lonely when I'm home, but I've been traveling so much I don't want him going between places."

Obi was sitting at Natalie's feet with his eyes wide, waiting for food.

"Something tells me that him sitting at your feet is not a new position for him."

Natalie shook her head. "I gave him a little bit and then Gina gave him a little bit, according to her. He's so spoiled now he turns his nose up at dog food."

Jackson smiled and looked at Natalie trying to give Obi a stern look and then tossing him a scrap of cheese. This is what he was missing. The smell of home. He liked taking Natalie out on dates but he had to admit being with her in her space was like no other.

He was old fashioned enough to like the idea she knew how to cook. More importantly, he liked being with Natalie. Even with Gina here it was still cozy. All the time he spent figuring out new businesses and making money didn't make up for the fact he wasn't around people outside of work. This last year it had been him and Obi. Standing in Natalie's kitchen he realized it had been lonelier than he knew.

He would treasure this time and use it as motivation to work for this to be the norm. Well, not the Gina part but definitely the Natalie and Obi part. If he had any doubts that this was what he wanted, those were all washed away when he sat down at the table. He wanted to do this every night with Natalie. As the realization settled in, Gina wasted no time in dishing out food.

"Jackson, I wanted to talk to you about Gran," Natalie said as they passed the bread basket around the table.

"Yes?"

"I think you need to work on the report you give her. She wasn't happy."

"I have to admit I wouldn't have been happy either, it was all fluff."

Gina passed the bowl of cheese around. "Can I even be at the table while you all discuss this?"

Jackson smiled. "There are no state secrets. I think that was the problem."

Natalie frowned. "She wanted to know you were making progress."

Jackson had several answers on his tongue. All of the responses would have been true but none of them would have made Natalie happy. He thought about riling her up just to see her get flushed in the cheeks and decide to lecture him on personnel 101, but here wasn't the place. So he did something he never did. Jackson Banner conceded a fight he knew could win.

"I'll take care of it when I see her next."

"Well, that ain't something you see every day," Gina said as she ate her lasagna, watching Jackson as she took each bite.

Jackson smiled at Gina. "It's not every day that I'm invited to a home-cooked meal."

"Is it something that you're looking to have in your life?"

Jackson gave Gina a smile and took a sip of the juice. "I could get used to it."

Natalie cleared her throat and looked at the both of them.

"Really? Any moment I expect you to get into the middle of the room and pull knives. If you want to get to dessert the both of you should pretend you like each other. Otherwise, Obi is going to be a very happy dog."

As if on cue Obi yipped and the tension that had been building in the air dissipated. Jackson held his hands up and smiled. "I give in. Having Obi upset with you is not pleasant."

"Natalie is interested in cooking and her career," Gina said sweetly. "You know they are thinking about making her an associate. It'll be a big coo for her."

"Is that right?" Jackson asked calmly.

Natalie looked at her plate very intently. "It's funny about communication and how it only works when both parties do it," Jackson said.

Natalie's head popped up. "I've been offered several things at my company but I haven't made any decisions. If there's no decisions then there isn't a need to have a conversation."

Then Natalie turned towards Gina. "Gina!"

"What?"

Jackson was confused about how he was talking to Natalie about the rest of their lives in one moment and in the next Gina was trying to look innocent at the table. Then he heard the sloppy chomping of Obi and lowered his head to hide his smile.

"Oh come on Natalie. He was starving," Gina protested.

"First of all, I don't think Obi has starved a day in his life," Natalie countered.

"I don't think you feel honored by the fact that he likes your food?" Jackson asked.

Natalie raised wrathful eyes towards him.

As the evening went on and dessert was served there were exclamations of how delicious the cheesecake was. The evening ended around nine. Jackson announced he was leaving and Natalie got up to walk him to the door. When they were standing there she was fidgeting and nervous.

"Thanks for coming by."

Jackson looked at her and thought she was still the most intriguing woman ever. She had kept him on his toes tonight and he learned that she may get upset, but it blew by quickly. When she extended her hand to say good night he looked at it and then slowly traveled up to meet her eyes.

Her breath was coming in short breaths and she had been worrying her bottom lips since she had shown him the door. He grabbed her hand and then leaned down and kissed her.

He felt her slight jump and then the transition into the kiss. He had agreed that they would be discreet, not dead. Besides, if the evening was any indication, Gina was already well aware of what he wanted and where this was going. Before she could protest he called out for Obi.

"Hey Obi, you have to slum it with the old man."

Obi looked longingly at Gina and then padded over to Jackson. Gina stood up and shook her head.

"I'll take him to your car," she said. "He can't walk so soon after eating."

Jackson didn't protest. He expected this because he understood Gina and she was a good friend of Natalie's.

The door closed and they had gone maybe two feet when Gina started.

"So, King-man what are you doing?" Gina asked.

"I think that's clear," Jackson replied calmly. "I'm getting back with Natalie."

"I heard you but I've known Natalie during one of your getting to know her moments. It doesn't usually work out well for her, if you know what I mean?"

"I know what you mean. A person has to answer for what they've done, and I was wrong."

"Really and that's it?"

They both walked to his car.

"I like you, Jackson. I just don't know if I like you for Natalie. She's special."

"You're right, you don't have a lot of reason to trust me. I'm working on it and all I can do is try to prove myself."

"Try?" Gina asked sarcastically.

Jackson sighed. "I expected this conversation with her parents or brother."

"Well, she doesn't have those. She's got me. So let's be clear. If you think you won't be able to cut it and go the whole way then don't start. It's not fair to her."

Gina handed him his dog and then left. He buckled Obi into his dog seat in the back and then drove to his home.

He understood that he had just promised Gina that he would be there for Natalie. When he thought about tomorrow it had her in it. The whole situation of her getting promoted would be one more thing they would have to work on. If the challenge didn't sway her, then he was ready for it.

Twenty-two

"Natalie help!" Elizabeth said.

"What's wrong?" Natalie said, already fiddling on her desk to find a pen and paper.

"Lori has taken out more money and she's made the checks out to a man named Marvin—"

"You've got to be kidding me. I know of him. Are you sure?"

"I had her followed, so yes, I'm sure. You've got to help her. If the old lady finds out, this will be the straw that breaks the camel's back. Please!"

Natalie couldn't believe her bad luck. Why didn't she have caller id? She tried to think of everything she could to stall to get Jackson. "Have you talked to her today?"

"I can't. Then I'll have to admit I had her followed because the transaction hasn't even hit the banks yet," Elizabeth snapped.

"If you know who this man is then you are the right person. This is something you can deal with at your level."

"At my level?"

"Yes go and see him and talk to him in the language that vile people like that understand."

"Elizabeth, I can't offer him money I don't have. Besides, I think it's safe to say that giving money is not the way."

"Well, I want Lori to stop selling her items and avoiding me. Fix it Natalie and call me when you're done." With that, Elizabeth hung up the phone.

Natalie looked at the deadline and couldn't believe she was in this spot again. She had barely been able to explain Chris. There would be no way to explain the Lori situation. She knew what she had to do but she was going to include Jackson this time.

She picked up her phone and texted, *Jackson?*

His response was instant, *Yes?*

I've got some personnel issues to address.

Do you need help?

For some reason his response comforted her, even if she didn't need his help, *No, I won't be alone.*

Good.

I'm just keeping you in the loop.

Thanks, be safe.

I won't be alone. I'll be with Lori.

A moment passed before his response came this time, *Lori?*

We should be fine I'll call if I need you.

K

Natalie wasn't feeling like the most honest person at the moment but she needed to see how bad it was. Maybe it wasn't as bad as she thought. She knew if she talked to him he would ask too many questions and she didn't have any answers. She called Lori next.

"Lori?"

"Yes?" Lori's voice was shaky and tremulous.

"Lori, it's me, Natalie. I wanted to talk to you. I'll be outside of your place in about an hour. Can you meet me at the Coffee shop on the corner?

"Why do you want to meet? I'm really busy today," Lori stated. "Is this about Jackson and his plans?"

Natalie thought about telling her the truth, but it seemed as though if she knew why she was coming, she'd run. So she went vague.

"I'm on my way and I'll explain then."

Natalie was shaking her head. Is this what her life had become?

"Where is she?" Jackson asked Catherine.

"She said she was going to take care of personnel issues and she had told you already."

Jackson was not going to lose it. He knew something was wrong but couldn't pinpoint it. When he received the text from Natalie he was in the middle of talking to his investigator who had given him all of the details he needed. When he was done with the investigator he wanted to see Nat right away, only to find that she was not in the office. He had confirmed the person who had been siphoning money from the organization and it didn't do anything to his peace of mind to know she was with Lori.

As soon as he got the information he knew Nat wasn't going to be happy. All of that was secondary to finding her.

Natalie had put on a blue top and black pants. She was glad that she had put those on now that she was in the coffee shop. She was accident prone when she was nervous and the colors would mask any spills. Still, she got her favorite coffee and sat down. Just as she was about to take a sip, Lori appeared in front of her.

She was wearing black from head to toe. It was on Natalie's lips to ask who had died, but she held her tongue and tried to put on a good face. Today instead of looking chic she looked tired and her eyes had dark circles beneath them.

"When do you have to see Marvin?" Natalie asked.

Lori's hand went to her mouth and she looked left and right as if she thought someone was following her. "How did you know?"

"Rob saw you with him and your mother has some suspicions as well," Natalie said. "This isn't like you Lori. Your mother is a mess with worry."

Lori dropped into the nearest stool. "Mother knows?" she asked forlornly.

Natalie nodded. "That, among other things, would be why I'm here."

"You don't understand Natalie. This is about family." Lori hung her head and stood up.

"Lori sit down. I will already have my hands full when I talk to Jackson. You've got to tell me everything so I can see what can be done."

Lori took a big breath and then let it out. "I have to do this and there isn't anything else to be done."

"Really Lori? I can't believe you'd steal from your own family," Natalie said disappointed.

"I'm not stealing from them. I'm stealing for them!" she hissed.

Natalie paused. "You know nothing is ever easy. Tell me."

Lori shook her head and then looked in her small bag until she pulled out a napkin.

"Marvin came by and told me that Chris had made a deal and he couldn't keep it. He was going to tell everyone that Chris broke his word and that he would tell his partners not to work with Connected unless I paid him the lost revenue.

"I've been taking the money out of jobs here and there but the amounts are getting bigger and bigger. I wanted to tell Chris but a couple of days ago he seemed like he was on top of the world and I love my brother too much to destroy his career."

"How long has this been going on, Lori?" Natalie asked in hushed tones. "And you haven't told anyone?"

"Who could I tell?" Lori asked sadly.

"It is amazing to me how much happens for the sake of the family. You all are so busy trying to protect each other but in the end you'd find talking to each other would be way more effective."

Lori nodded and she looked away as she wallowed in her own despair.

"Well, Lori blackmailers rarely go away on their own. They stay until they bleed you dry."

"I know but I don't see any options."

"Hold on one moment," Natalie said and grabbed her phone out of her purse.

Jackson?

Nat where are you?

With Lori.

I need you back at the office.

Really? Natalie couldn't help but wonder why, *I'll be there in an hour.*

Are you okay?

Yes, I have to do one thing and I'll be there.

Natalie put her phone away and then turned back to Lori.

"So it seems like you are the person that Jackson has been looking for."

"I've been trying to find other ways to get the money so no one will notice," Lori said.

"Well, the bad news is everyone has noticed. The good news is only the family knows."

Lori let her head fall to the tabletop. "He's going to put me in jail, and he'll go to Gran."

Natalie paused and looked at Lori's head on the table. For a moment she couldn't tell what was distressing her more, going to jail or telling Gran.

Natalie tapped the tabletop. "Come on Lori, we have to get ourselves together so we can get through this."

"We can't," Lori moaned.

"First we are going to do what everyone does with bullies."

"Pay him off," Lori said.

"No, we're going to threaten him with a bigger bully!"

She was going to kill him. She had called him and told him that Gina was on assignment and they could meet at her house. She began to tell him the story while she heated up the lasagna.

This is what being in love with Natalie would be like. She fought for the weak and gave no thought to herself. It was a little scary how much faith she had in him.

"So before you tell me the story can you answer some questions?"

Natalie smiled at him while she stirred the pot.

"Where were you today?" Jackson asked in the calmest voice he had.

Natalie smiled and looked at him over her shoulder. "I had to help Lori, which is what I wanted to talk to you about."

"Ah, did you get my text?"

"I did Jackson and I responded."

"Yes, you said personnel issues."

"Yes, so let me tell you."

Jackson listened to her tell the story and several times, when he thought of how dangerous Marvin could be, he had to hold on to the table thinking about how he could have lost her.

"That was that and I told him he was going to have to deal with you."

"Nat, I think we need to talk."

She looked up and it was like she was seeing him for the first time for the night. "Jackson, what's wrong?"

"What's wrong is you weren't very clear on what you were doing today. Today you put yourself in danger."

"I did what I had to do. I knew you'd take care of it."

"Nat, it's not the money. Money, I can make all day long."

Natalie got up. "I'm not hungry."

Jackson stood so they were face to face. When she went to sidestep him he pulled her into his embrace.

"Jackson?"

He knew she could feel the tremor that went through his body. "Ah Queenie, I can make money without thinking but you are irreplaceable." He pulled back and leaned in to kiss her. He kissed her thinking about the days that had passed. He deepened his kiss thinking about meals in the future. When he lifted his head to look at her. Her lips were swollen, her eyes were half-closed and her arms were wrapped around his neck as if he were the only anchor for her to hold onto.

She looked at him and cupped his face and leaned in to kiss him again. When she pulled back she said, "I didn't know. I'm sorry. I only thought about Lori."

"I love how selfless you are, but I don't think I'm going to survive you being there for everyone," he said with a laugh.

"What did you say?"

"I said that your spirit is—"

Natalie held up her hand and gave him a stern look. "Try again with the L-word."

Jackson smiled. "The thing that everyone knows is, I love you, Natalie. I know we have things we need to address. You've got a career. I've got a company. We've got a dog. I'm ready this time. We can work it out. Besides if anything goes wrong you do know Gina has threatened me right?"

Natalie laughed. "Gina is some serious business."

Keys jangled and the door opened. Natalie looked over Jackson's shoulder.

"Finally! Tell me one of you really smart people have gotten it together." Gina said as she closed the door.

"Yes, we've got it together," Jackson said smiling at Natalie.

"Well, I just want you to know while the love glow is on you both. I'm not moving, so think about that. Rent is a killer in this neighborhood," Gina muttered as she went into the back.

"So not to be technical here but you haven't said it," Jackson said as he looked into Natalie's eyes.

"Said what?"

"Really?"

"Oh, yes, well you already know so there's no need in saying it," she teased.

"Natalie?"

"I love you, Jackson. I've always loved you. I wasn't sure if I could trust the feeling but I've always loved you."

"WOO HOO!" Gina yelled from the back.

"So do you think we can go public now?" Jackson asked.

"Yeah, I think you're good for it," she replied.

Jackson smiled and thought about how this was the beginning of a life that only love could buy.

Epilogue

A man had to be able to admit when he was wrong. Looking at Gina Kenyon standing with her friend Natalie Tucker, Christopher Griggs was calling himself all types of names. Chris didn't usually accept invites from other businessmen without his lawyers. However, Jackson Banner was a man he respected as well as the owner of a company he had thought about acquiring. Chris had broken his habit and come here tonight for one reason, Gina Kenyon.

Gina Kenyon was the one that got away. As it turned out, she was the one he couldn't do without. Gina was the epitome of kindness and one of the most giving women he had ever met, but his pride had gotten the best of him.

Natalie Tucker was leaving Vision Consulting, and Gina was taking on her projects. This was a passing of the baton party. Gina had her dark hair pulled back into a bun. She stood next to her friend, Natalie, patiently talking to everyone who approached her. That was Gina. She didn't turn you away and when she spoke to you, it was as if no one else in the world existed. She had shown him what it means to be appreciated for himself. She had accepted him on face value and never asked for anything in return.

He had to make it right. He was used to challenges. Chris was used to people saying something couldn't be done, and he'd accomplish it anyway. He was going to have to bring all of those skills he learned in business to be face this new challenge. When it came to winning back Gina's heart, failure wasn't option not if he ever wanted to be whole again.

I hope you enjoyed Natalie and Jackson's story. If you'd like to read more about the women in Vision Consulting and the men who are looking for a second chance with them. Check out *Love Me* for book two of the Love Endures series and read Gina's story. If you've enjoyed reading this book, please take a moment to write a review.

Sign up to my newsletter to receive updates on new releases, sale promotions, and free books.

susanwarnerauthor.com

Here's a peek at book 2

LOVE *Me*

One

Gina Kenyon had come a long way to find a thief. Christopher Griggs might be a CEO, but if the thief shoe fit, she was sure going to make him wear it. There weren't words for his blatant boldness of hoodwinkery. She didn't even know if that was a word, but it didn't matter. What mattered was this morning,

Gina had walked into Cora Thalman's office, her boss at Vision Consulting, and was handed a project. That, in and of itself, wasn't an issue. She was one of the best project managers in the company. It wasn't an issue when Cora told her that Vision needed to get this account. Mr. Griggs had already sent back three project managers. The problem was it was her project. She had put in her hard work and time to create it. Gina's project plans were distinctive in the detail and efficiency, so much so she didn't understand how anyone thought they could steal one.

Mr. Griggs had a lot to answer for. It was bad enough there was only one place he could have gotten the project from—but she didn't want to think about that because that was a mistake she was desperately trying to forget.

Griggs owned Chymera Corporations. It was known for eating up little companies and adding it to their conglomerate or dismantling companies that were in its way. Chymera worked in the tech industries and government contracts.

Gina tried to remember the calming conversation she had practiced with her friend, Natalie. Natalie was always trying to help her with ways to keep calm. She needed to practice being calm before she met the thief who was trying to abscond with her work.

Gina tried to give him the benefit of the doubt as she walked through the front doors of the New Hope Center. Maybe Griggs wasn't the thieving person she thought he was.

When she stepped into the foyer, the first thing she noticed was an older woman sitting at a desk with what looked like large butterflies in her hair. Gina could see the coiled springs that kept the wings attached and moving with every movement of the woman's head and every breeze that went through the foyer.

"Can I help you?" the older woman asked. Gina pulled her gaze away from the bright butterflies and tried to find the words to respond. Now that she was up close, it was clear that the butterflies were perched in auburn hair that was definitely attached to a wig. Gina could tell as it was just a smidgen off-Center, leaving a little bit of the woman's natural hair exposed.

Gina supposed she was taking too long to answer, and then the woman reached up and touched the exposed spot and then laughed.

"Don't worry, I know it's peeking out. It was itching this morning, and I gave up. Decided that I'm old enough to do what I want, and my comfort was way more important than the look. What can I do for you?"

Gina walked closer to the desk, pulled in by the woman's smile.

"I'm here to see Mr. Griggs," Gina said with a smile of her own.

The woman transformed right before her. Where there had been a smiling woman who was undoubtedly someone's grandmother, sat an angry woman with pursed lips and little patience. She crossed her arms in front of her chest and gave Gina a narrowed gazed.

"You? With him?" she asked incredulously.

"He asked me to meet him here," Gina replied.

"My name is Daisy. You look like a nice girl," Daisy said as if seeing Griggs and being a nice girl was a total contradiction.

A door opened on the left, and out came a small man, about five foot two with grey hair. He had a thin frame and an easy smile.

He walked behind the desk, and Daisy looked at him.

"Tim, she's here to see Griggs."

Tim looked Gina over from head to toe and shook his head before speaking.

"I guess you can't tell anymore. She looks like such a nice girl," he murmured.

Gina was about to comment when she saw Daisy reach over to her phone and then call out. "Griggs, come out here!"

Gina didn't have time to be shocked because the same door that Tim had come through slammed open, and a tall, handsome man stepped into the foyer.

"You!" exclaimed Gina.

The man looked up to see Gina and sucked his teeth. "This day just isn't going to get any be better."

"Well, I guess you shouldn't expect good things when you steal," Gina spat back. She turned back to Daisy. "Call Mr. Griggs; he'll want to know about this man."

Daisy and Tim looked confused and didn't move. Gina got ready to explain when he spoke.

"Gina, my full name is Christopher Alex Myers Griggs. Myers is my mother's maiden name."

Gina turned back to Christopher and tried to comprehend what was going on.

"You're Griggs, and you're Myers?" This day was just spiraling out of control. Gina had been primed to tell the CEO, Mr. Griggs, that he had some gall to request her to implement the plan he stole from her company. Now that she had met Mr. Griggs, it was all clear.

The man before her she knew as Alex Myers, the nice man she attended the project management classes with for the last year and a half. Then he just disappeared. No notice, no warning just got up and left. She had thought she and Alex were getting close, but when he just disappeared, she tried to toss it up as one of those things.

Now she knew how Mr. Griggs had gotten her project. This project was the one they had both worked on in class together. He hadn't just disappeared. He had stolen their project, and now here he was.

"Yes, if you will come with me, I'll explain—" Christopher said as he was cut off by Daisy.

"I bet he will," Daisy said with a snort.

"Don't fall for his foolishness, girl. You seem really nice," Tim chimed in.

Gina knew her face was set in grim resolution as she walked through the door. She followed him down the hall and tried to focus. It didn't matter what his name was. She knew what he was. He was six feet of well-muscled predator. The charcoal gray suit he wore couldn't hide that raw, animal aura that surrounded him. It wasn't just his jet black hair and hypnotic sable brown eyes, it was the man himself that first attracted her to him a year ago before he broke her heart.

They walked down the hall into an office, and when she stepped in, she turned and eyed him cautiously as he closed the door. She could feel her heart beating faster and her breath coming in short rasps. What was wrong with her? This man—no matter what his name—was a trickster, a fake, a thief, and an opportunist. However, even knowing what she knew, he still had the power to make her uneasy. It didn't help that she was five feet, eight inches. It meant that on top of everything else, he could loom over her.

"So whoever you are, I'm sure you can come up with a good story for all of this," Gina stated. Gina didn't have a family, she was a product of multiple foster homes. None of them were bad, they just weren't family, and they weren't hers. Sometimes she thought this was why she didn't play well with others.

"I told you who I am," Christopher said. "I need you to listen to me, so I can explain."

"Explain? Why should I listen? What new story will you spin now?" Gina balled her hands into fists to stop herself from giving in to the silky tones that seemed to wrap themselves around herself resolve. What was wrong with her? She knew he couldn't be trusted. No man had ever had this effect on her. Of all people, why did it have to be him she had to deal with now?

"I made a mistake. Okay, I made a bunch of mistakes," Christopher murmured softly.

"Mistakes? Not very original for a CEO. Listen, the past is the past. Why am I here?"

"I've been trying to find the best way to contact you and explain. In the end, I thought this would be the best way. I also need your help."

"You lie to me, steal my work, and now you need my help?" she asked incredulously.

"Hear me out," he said with his hands up.

Her brain was saying walk out the door and go home. Unfortunately, it seemed that organ wasn't in control. Gina had to admit Christopher was easy on the eyes and could talk a smooth game. It was his eyes. When he fixed them on her, she could feel a coil of excitement unfurl in her. She wanted to look away, but she wouldn't give him the satisfaction of knowing he unnerved her in any way. She felt like Little Red Riding Hood, and the wolf was inviting her to dinner at his place to talk.

"Everyone gets a free consultation hour. If you want to waste yours trying to explain, go right ahead," Gina said, tucking a strand of hair behind her ear.

"You know I own Chymera corp."

"I know now," Gina muttered.

"Well, I do, and we acquire, dismantle, or absorb companies. It's old, and I wanted to do something new. I bought this Health Center about a year and a half ago."

Gina looked around the office they were in. The walls were grey with time and a dusting of dirt. The floor was old linoleum just like the front, and the furniture looked as though it had been salvaged from what the garage sales wouldn't take. Two fold-up chairs against the wall. A wooden desk that, if she wasn't mistaken, had a tilt to it as if one of the legs was a bit short.

"Well, you haven't left much of a mark around here. No one would mistake this for one of your businesses in the city."

Christopher sat down in the chair, and for a moment, Gina held her breath, unsure if the chair was strong enough to hold him, if it wasn't she would find herself having to pick him up from the floor.

"That was the point. I used all of the techniques I had always used, and nothing I did here seemed to help. My COO is my sister Gwen. She looked at this place and said it was a waste and that I was wasting my money."

"So, this place is a dare for you?"

Christopher sighed. "It might have been when I bought it, but I've been here with them for the last year, and they've grown on me. It's true it's an acquired taste. Even Daisy at the front has grown on me, but I have to tell you, Healthcare isn't the same as business, and the things I know don't translate the way I wanted. So I went back to school. I took a course using my middle and mother's maiden name. I made sure it was at night, and then I met you."

"For a year, Alex! Or Chris, or whatever! You couldn't tell me during the year we dated?" Gina asked.

"The truth of it was I thought things would change if you knew I had money."

"Did I seem that shallow?"

"NO!"

"Maybe I seemed like a money-grubber?"

"No, Gina never."

"Then maybe—"

"It wasn't you. It was me."

"Oh, we've all heard that one before Chris—"

"I enjoyed being with you," Chris said softly. "Gina, you're bold, direct, and beautiful. You make no apologies for your thoughts, and you always say it straight and—"

"After two semesters and us doing a project, which just so happens to be in healthcare, you disappeared and then stole my project!"

Chris stood up and held his arms wide. "When you say it like that, it sounds bad. It didn't happen like that for me, but I can see—"

"Can you see why I'm thinking the smart thing to do is to walk out the door, Chris? Can you see that?" she said with her hand on her hip and her shoe tapping away.

Chris stopped and looked at her. "I can see we are about to negotiate."

Gina stood under his gaze for a moment and tried hard not to fidget and to hold on to her anger. Why was he watching her like that? She wanted to touch her hair and smooth her clothing. What was he looking at so intently? Then when she saw the light, male interest in his eye, she stood a little taller and squared her shoulders. She wasn't his height, but she wouldn't slump or hide. She walked boldly to his chair and looked down at him.

"You don't have anything I want."

Chris stood up and moved the chair aside. It took all of two seconds for him to turn the tables on her. "I'm sorry, Gina. I was wrong. Let's start over."

When did his lips become so intriguing? She closed her eyes and took a breath.

"You're wasting your time," she said through clenched teeth.

"What if I told you I wanted you to reconsider staying for the Center's sake and not mine?"

Gina looked at him sideways and remembered an article she had read about him. In it, they called him The Closer. He was living up to that title today. He was a hawk, watching every movement she made.

Being this close to him gave her a better view of him as well. Chris was impressive in the distance, but up close and personal, he was a force of nature. She could feel power radiating off of him and sending shivers down her spine.

"Don't you think that's a bit of a reach even for you?" This close, he was making her nervous. She was confused by the conflicting signs and feelings that she was trying to manage while presenting a cool façade to Chris.

"What I think is I screwed up. I might have thought what I did was for the right reasons, but I was wrong. Give me a month. Get to know me and let me show you who I really am. I'm asking for a chance, and while we're here, we can help this Center."

Gina played the offer around in her head. It was a plan she knew. This was an account she knew her boss said she had to get, and it was in a field she excelled in.

"Just out of curiosity, how would you explain me to everyone?"

Chris' smile widened. "I'll take care of that. Do we have a deal?"

Make a deal with Christopher. What was she thinking? Better yet, what she didn't need to be thinking about was how sexy his voice was. Gina could feel sparks racing along her body as his smooth voice undulated through her. Of all the men to finally have a reaction to, it had to be him!

Not one to back down from a fight or leave others in need, Gina already knew her answer. She looked up at him and glowered.

"I'll stay for the Center, and when I'm done, I'm done. Nothing more between you and me. You lied to me, and I don't think I can trust you. Take it or leave it."

Chris smiled and nodded. "I'll take...you—I mean, I accept your deal."

"Dream on Mr. CEO. I'm here for the Center. I'll call to contact you in a couple of days to start." She didn't wait for a response. Instead, she stepped away and walked out of the Center. When she got back to her car, she looked at the Center and sighed.

"Gina girl, what have you done?"